MURDER
IN ANY DEGREE

Owen Johnson

1st WORLD
LIBRARY
Literary Society

Murder in Any Degree

Owen Johnson

© 1st World Library – Literary Society, 2005
PO Box 2211
Fairfield, IA 52556
www.1stworldlibrary.org
First Edition

LCCN: 2004195655

Softcover ISBN: 1-4218-0476-X
Hardcover ISBN: 1-4218-0376-3
eBook ISBN: 1-4218-0576-6

Purchase *"Murder in Any Degree"*
as a traditional bound book at:
www.1stWorldLibrary.org/purchase.asp?ISBN=1-4218-0476-X

1st World Library Literary Society is a nonprofit
organization dedicated to promoting literacy by:

- Creating a free internet library accessible from any
  computer worldwide.
- Hosting writing competitions and offering book
  publishing scholarships.

Murder in Any Degree
contributed by Tim, Ed & Rodney
in support of
1st World Library Literary Society

Murder in Any Degree
contributed by Tim, Ed & Rodney
in support of
1st World Library Literary Society

CONTENTS

MURDER IN ANY DEGREE

I

One Sunday in March they had been marooned at the club, Steingall the painter and Quinny the illustrator, and, having lunched late, had bored themselves separately to their limits over the periodicals until, preferring to bore each other, they had gravitated together in easy arm-chairs before the big Renaissance fireplace.

Steingall, sunk in his collar, from behind the black-rimmed spectacles, which, with their trailing ribbon of black, gave a touch of Continental elegance to his cropped beard and colonel's mustaches, watched without enthusiasm the three mammoth logs, where occasional tiny flames gave forth an illusion of heat.

Quinny, as gaunt as a militant friar of the Middle Ages, aware of Steingall's protective reverie, spoke in desultory periods, addressing himself questions and supplying the answers, reserving his epigrams for a larger audience.

At three o'clock De Gollyer entered from a heavy social performance, raising his eyebrows in salute as others raise their hats, and slightly dragging one leg behind. He was an American critic who was busily engaged in discovering the talents of unrecognized geniuses of the European provinces. When reproached with his migratory enthusiasm, he would reply, with that quick, stiffening military click with which he always delivered his *bons mots*:

"My boy, I never criticize American art. I can't afford to. I have too many charming friends."

At four o'clock, which is the hour for the entree of those who escape from their homes to fling themselves on the sanctuary of the club, Rankin, the architect, arrived with Stibo, the fashionable painter of fashionable women, who brought with him the atmosphere of pleasant soap and an exclusive, smiling languor. A moment later a voice was heard from the anteroom, saying:

"If any one telephones, I'm not in the club - any one at all. Do you hear?"

Then Towsey, the decorator, appeared at the letterboxes in spats, militant checks, high collar and a choker tie, which, yearning toward his ears, gave him the appearance of one who had floundered up out of his clothes for the third and last time. He came forward, frowned at the group, scowled at the negative distractions of the reading-room, and finally dragged over his chair just as Quinny was saying:

"Queer thing - ever notice it? - two artists sit down together, each begins talking of what he's doing - to avoid complimenting the other, naturally. As soon as the third arrives they begin carving up another; only thing they can agree on, see? Soon as you get four or more of the species together , conversation always

Owen Johnson

comes around to marriage. Ever notice that, eh?"

"My dear fellow," said De Gollyer, from the intolerant point of view of a bachelor, "that is because marriage is your one common affliction. Artists, musicians, all the lower order of the intellect, marry. They must. They can't help it. It's the one thing you can't resist. You begin it when you're poor to save the expense of a servant, and you keep it up when you succeed to have some one over you to make you work. You belong psychologically to the intellectually dependent classes, the clinging-vine family, the masculine parasites; and as you can't help being married, you are always damning it, holding it responsible for all your failures."

At this characteristic speech, the five artists shifted slightly, and looked at De Gollyer over their mustaches with a lingering appetite, much as a group of terriers respect the family cat.

"My dear chaps, speaking as a critic," continued De Gollyer, pleasantly aware of the antagonism he had exploded, "you remain children afraid of the dark - afraid of being alone. Solitude frightens you. You lack the quality of self-sufficiency that is the characteristic of the higher critical faculties. You marry because you need a nurse."

He ceased, thoroughly satisfied with the prospect of having brought on a quarrel, raised thumb and first finger in a gingerly loop, ordered a dash of sherry and winked across the group to Tommers, who was listening around his paper from the reading-room.

"De Gollyer, you are only a 'who's who' of art," said Quinny, with, however, a hungry gratitude for a topic of such possibilities. "You understand nothing of psychology. An artist is a multiple personality; with each picture he paints he seeks a new inspiration. What is inspiration?"

"Ah, that's the point - inspiration," said Steingall, waking up.

"Inspiration," said Quinny, eliminating Steingall from his preserves with the gesture of brushing away a fly - "inspiration is only a form of hypnosis, under the spell of which a man is capable of rising outside of and beyond himself, as a horse, under extraordinary stress, exerts a muscular force far beyond his accredited strength. The race of geniuses, little and big, are constantly seeking this outward force to hypnotize them into a supreme intellectual effort. Talent does not understand such a process; it is mechanical, unvarying, chop-chop, day in and day out. Now, what you call inspiration may be communicated in many ways - by the spectacle of a mob, by a panorama of nature, by sudden and violent contrasts of points of view; but, above all, as a continual stimulus, it comes from that state of mental madness which is produced by love."

"Huh?" said Stibo.

"Anything that produces a mental obsession, *une idee fixe*, is a form of madness," said Quinny, rapidly. "A person in love sees only one face, hears only one voice; at the base of the brain only one thought is constantly drumming. Physically such a condition is a narcotic; mentally it is a form of madness that in the beneficent state is powerfully hypnotic."

At this deft disentanglement of a complicated idea,

Owen Johnson

Rankin, who, like the professional juryman, wagged his head in agreement with each speaker and was convinced by the most violent, gazed upon Quinny with absolute adoration.

"We were speaking of woman," said Towsey, gruffly, who pronounced the sex with a peculiar staccato sound.

"This little ABC introduction," said Quinny, pleasantly, "is necessary to understand the relation a woman plays to the artist. It is not the woman he seeks, but the hypnotic influence which the woman can exert on his faculties if she is able to inspire him with a passion."

"Precisely why he marries," said De Gollyer.

"Precisely," said Quinny, who, having seized the argument by chance, was pleasantly surprised to find that he was going to convince himself. "But here is the great distinction: to be an inspiration, a woman should always represent to the artist a form of the unattainable. It is the search for something beyond him that makes him challenge the stars, and all that sort of rot, you know."

"The tragedy of life," said Rankin, sententiously, "is that one woman cannot mean all things to one man all the time."

It was a phrase which he had heard the night before, and which he flung off casually with an air of spontaneity, twisting the old Spanish ring on his bony, white fingers, which he held invariably in front of his long, sliding nose.

"Thank you, I said that about the year 1907," said Quinny, while Steingall gasped and nudged Towsey. "That is the tragedy of life, not the tragedy of art, two very different things. An artist has need of ten, fifteen, twenty women, according to the multiplicity of his ideas. He should be always violently in love or violently reacting."

"And the wife?" said De Gollyer. "Has she any influence?"

"My dear fellow, the greatest. Without a wife, an artist falls a prey to the inspiration of the moment - condemned to it; and as he is not an analyst, he ends by imagining he really is in love. Take portrait-painting. Charming lady sits for portrait, painter takes up his brushes, arranges his palette, seeks inspiration, - what is below the surface? - something intangible to divine, seize, and affix to his canvas. He seeks to know the soul; he seeks how? As a man in love seeks, naturally. The more he imagines himself in love, the more completely does the idea obsess him from morning to night - plain as the nose on your face. Only there are other portraits to paint. Enter the wife."

"Charming," said Stibo, who had not ceased twining his mustaches in his pink fingers.

"Ah, that's the point. What of the wife?" said Steingall, violently.

"The wife - the ideal wife, mind you - is then the weapon, the refuge. To escape from the entanglement of his momentary inspiration, the artist becomes a man: my wife and *bonjour*. He returns home, takes off the duster of his illusion, cleans the palette of old memories, washes away his vows, protestations, and all that rot, you know, lies down on the sofa, and gives his head to his wife to be rubbed. Curtain. The comedy is over."

"But that's what they don't understand," said Steingall, with enthusiasm. "That's what they will *never* understand."

"Such miracles exist?" said Towsey with a short, disagreeable laugh.

"I know the wife of an artist," said Quinny, "whom I consider the most remarkable woman I know - who sits and knits and smiles. She is one who understands. Her husband adores her, and he is in love with a woman a month. When he gets in too deep, ready for another inspiration, you know, she calls up the old love on the telephone and asks her to stop annoying her husband."

"Marvelous!" said Steingall, dropping his glasses.

"No, really?" said Rankin.

"Has she a sister?" said Towsey.

Stibo raised his eyes slowly to Quinny's but veiled as was the look, De Gollyer perceived it, and smilingly registered the knowledge on the ledger of his social secrets.

"That's it, by George! that is it," said Steingall, who hurled the enthusiasm of a reformer into his pessimism. "It's all so simple; but they won't understand. And why - do you know why? Because a woman is jealous. It isn't simply of other women. No, no, that's not it; it's worse than that, ten thousand times worse. She's jealous of your *art*! That's it! There you have it! She's jealous because she can't understand it, because it takes you away from her, because she can't *share* it. That's what's terrible about marriage - no liberty, no individualism, no seclusion, having to account every night for your actions, for your thoughts, for the things you dream - ah, the dreams! The Chinese are right, the Japanese are right. It's we Westerners who are all wrong. It's the creative only that counts. The woman should be subordinated, should be kept down, taught the voluptuousness of obedience. By Jove! that's it. We don't assert ourselves. It's this confounded Anglo-Saxon sentimentality that's choking art - that's what it is."

At the familiar phrases of Steingall's outburst, Rankin wagged his head in unequivocal assent, Stibo smiled so as to show his fine upper teeth, and Towsey flung away his cigar, saying:

"Words, words."

At this moment when Quinny, who had digested Steingall's argument, was preparing to devour the whole topic, Britt Herkimer, the sculptor, joined them. He was a guest, just in from Paris, where he had been established twenty years, one of the five men in art whom one counted on the fingers when the word genius was pronounced. Mentally and physically a German, he spoke English with a French accent. His hair was cropped *en brosse*, and in his brown Japanese face only the eyes, staccato, furtive, and drunk with curiosity, could be seen. He was direct, opinionated, bristling with energy, one of those tireless workers who disdain their youth and treat it as a disease. His entry into the group of his more socially domesticated confreres was like the return of a wolf-hound among the housedogs.

"Still smashing idols?" he said, slapping the shoulder of Steingall, with whom and Quinny he had passed his student days, "Well, what's the row?"

"My dear Britt, we are reforming matrimony. Steingall is for the importation of Mongolian wives," said De Gollyer, who had written two favorable articles on Herkimer, "while Quinny is for founding a school for wives on most novel and interesting lines."

"That's odd," said Herkimer, with a slight frown.

"On the contrary, no," said De Gollyer; "we always abolish matrimony from four to six."

"You didn't understand me," said Herkimer, with the sharpness he used in his classes.

From his tone the group perceived that the hazards had brought to him some abrupt coincidence. They waited with an involuntary silence, which in itself was a rare tribute.

"Remember Rantoul?" said Herkimer, rolling a cigarette and using a jerky diction.

"Clyde Rantoul?" said Stibo.

"Don Furioso Barebones Rantoul, who in the Quarter with us?" said Quinny.

"Don Furioso, yes," said Rankin. "Ever see him?"

"Never."

"He's married," said Quinny; "dropped out."

"Yes, he married," said Herkimer, lighting his cigarette. "Well, I've just seen him."

"He's a plutocrat or something," said Towsey, reflectively.

"He's rich - ended," said Steingall as he slapped the table. "By Jove! I remember now."

"Wait," said Quinny, interposing.

"I went up to see him yesterday - just back now," said Herkimer. "Rantoul was the biggest man of us all. It's a funny tale. You're discussing matrimony; here it is."

II

In the early nineties, when Quinny, Steingall, Herkimer, little Bennett, who afterward roamed down into the Transvaal and fell in with the Foreign Legion, Jacobus and Chatterton, the architects, were living through that fine, rebellious state of overweening youth, Rantoul was the undisputed leader, the arch-rebel, the master-demolisher of the group.

Every afternoon at five his Gargantuan figure came thrashing through the crowds of the boulevard, as an omnibus on its way scatters the fragile fiacres. He arrived, radiating electricity, tirades on his tongue, to his chair among the table-pounders of the Cafe des Lilacs, and his first words were like the fanfare of trumpets. He had been christened, in the felicitous language of the Quarter, Don Furioso Barebones Rantoul, and for cause. He shared a garret with his chum, Britt Herkimer, in the Rue de l'Ombre, a sort of manhole lit by the stars, - when there were any stars, and he never failed to come springing up the six rickety flights with a song on his lips.

An old woman who kept a fruit store gave him implicit credit; a much younger member of the sex at the corner creamery trusted him for eggs and fresh milk, and leaned toward him over the counter, laughing into his eyes as he exclaimed:

"Ma belle, when I am famous, I will buy you a silk gown, and a pair of earrings that will reach to your shoulders, and it won't be long. You'll see."

He adored being poor. When his canvas gave out, he painted his ankles to caricature the violent creations that were the pride of Chatterton, who was a nabob. When his credit at one restaurant expired, he strode confidently up to another proprietor, and announced with the air of one bestowing a favor:

"I am Rantoul, the portrait-painter. In five years my portraits will sell for five thousand francs, in ten for twenty thousand. I will eat one meal a day at your distinguished establishment, and paint your portrait to make your walls famous. At the end of the month I will immortalize your wife; on the same terms, your sister, your father, your mother, and all the little children. Besides, every Saturday night I will bring here a band of my comrades who pay in good hard silver. Remember that if you had bought a Corot for twenty francs in 1870, you could have sold it for five thousand francs in 1880, fifty thousand in 1890. Does the idea appeal to you?"

But as most keepers of restaurants are practical and unimaginative, and withal close bargainers, at the end of a week Rantoul generally was forced to seek a new sitter.

"What a privilege it is to be poor!" he would then exclaim enthusiastically to Herkimer. "It awakens all the perceptions; hunger makes the eye keener. I can see colors to-day that I never saw before. And to think that if Sherman had never gotten it in his head to march to the sea I should never have experienced this

　　　　　Owen Johnson

inspiration! But, old fellow, we have so short a time to be poor. We must exhibit nothing yet. We are lucky. We are poor. We can feel."

On the subject of traditions he was at his best.

"Shakspere is the curse of the English drama," he would declare, with a descending gesture which caused all the little glasses to rattle their alarm. "Nothing will ever come out of England until his influence is discounted. He was a primitive, a Preraphaelite. He understood nothing of form, of composition. He was a poet who wandered into the drama as a sheep strays into the pasture of the bulls, a colorist who imagines he can be a sculptor. The influence of Victoria sentimentalized the whole artistic movement in England, made it bourgeois, and flavored it with mint sauce. Modern portraiture has turned the galleries into an exhibition of wax works. What is wrong with painting to-day - do you know?"

"*Allons*, tell us!" cried two or three, while others, availing themselves of the breathing space, filled the air with their orders:

"Paul, another bock."

"Two hard-boiled eggs."

"And pretzels; don't forget the pretzels."

"The trouble with painting to-day is that it has no point of view," cried Rantoul, swallowing an egg in the anaconda fashion. "We are interpreting life in the manner of the Middle Ages. We forget art should be historical. We forget that we are now in our century.

Ugliness, not beauty, is the note of our century; turbulence, strife, materialism, the mob, machinery, masses, not units. Why paint a captain of industry against a Francois I tapestry? Paint him at his desk. The desk is a throne; interpret it. We are ruled by mobs. Who paints mobs? What is wrong is this, that art is in the bondage of literature - sentimentality. We must record what we experience. Ugliness has its utility, its magnetism; the ugliness of abject misery moves you to think, to readjust ideas. We must be rebels, we young men. Ah, if we could only burn the galleries, we should be forced to return to life."

"Bravo, Rantoul!"

"Right, old chap."

"Smash the statues!"

"Burn the galleries!"

"Down with tradition!"

"Eggs and more bock!"

But where Rantoul differed from the revolutionary regiment was that he was not simply a painter who delivered orations; he could paint. His tirades were not a furore of denunciation so much as they were the impulsive chafing of the creative energy within him. In the school he was already a marked man to set the prophets prophesying. He had a style of his own, biting, incisive, overloaded and excessive, but with something to say. He was after something. He was original.

Owen Johnson

"Rebel! Let us rebel!" he would cry to Herkimer from his agitated bedquilt in the last hour of discussion. "The artist must always rebel - accept nothing, question everything, denounce conventions and traditions."

"Above all, work," said Herkimer in his laconic way.

"What? Don't I work?"

"Work more."

Rantoul, however, was not vulnerable on that score. He was not, it is true, the drag-horse that Herkimer was, who lived like a recluse, shunning the cafes and the dance-halls, eating up the last gray hours of the day over his statues and his clays. But Rantoul, while living life to its fullest, haunting the wharves and the markets with avid eyes, roaming the woods and trudging the banks of the Seine, mingling in the crowds that flashed under the flare of arc-lights, with a thousand mysteries of mass and movement, never relaxed a moment the savage attack his leaping nature made upon the drudgeries and routine of technic.

With the coveted admittance into the Salon, recognition came speedily to the two chums. They made a triumphal entry into a real studio in the Montparnasse Quarter, clients came, and the room became a station of honor among the young and enthusiastic of the Quarter.

Rantoul began to appear in society, besieged with the invitations that his Southern aristocracy and the romance of his success procured him.

"You go out too much," said Herkimer to him, with a fearful growl. "What the deuce do you want with society, anyhow? Keep away from it. You've nothing to do with it."

"What do I do? I go out once a week," said Rantoul, whistling pleasantly.

"Once is too often. What do you want to become, a parlor celebrity? Society *c'est l'ennemie*. You ought to hate it."

"I do."

"Humph!" said Herkimer, eying him across his sputtering clay pipe. "Get this idea of people out of your head. Shut yourself up in a hole, work. What's society, anyhow? A lot of bored people who want you to amuse them. I don't approve. Better marry that pretty girl in the creamery. She'll worship you as a god, make you comfortable. That's all you need from the world."

"Marry her yourself; she'll sew and cook for you," said Rantoul, with perfect good humor.

"I'm in no danger," said Herkimer, curtly; "you are."

"What!"

"You'll see."

"Listen, you old grumbler," said Rantoul, seriously. "If I go into society, it is to see the hollowness of it all - "

"Yes, yes."

"To know what I rebel against - "

"Of course."

"To appreciate the freedom of the life I have - "

"Faker!"

"To have the benefit of contrasts, light and shade. You think I am not a rebel. My dear boy, I am ten times as big a rebel as I was. Do you know what I'd do with society?"

He began a tirade in the famous muscular Rantoul style, overturning creeds and castes, reorganizing republics and empires, while Herkimer, grumbling to himself, began to scold the model, who sleepily received the brunt of his ill humor.

In the second year of his success Rantoul, quite by accident, met a girl in her teens named Tina Glover, only daughter of Cyrus Glover, a man of millions, self-made. The first time their eyes met and lingered, by the mysterious chemistry of the passions Rantoul fell desperately in love with this little slip of a girl, who scarcely reached to his shoulder; who, on her part, instantly made up her mind that she had found the husband she intended to have. Two weeks later they were engaged.

She was seventeen, scarcely more than a child, with clear, blue eyes that seemed too large for her body, very timid and appealing. It is true she seldom expressed an opinion, but she listened to every one with a flattering smile, and the reputations of brilliant talkers have been built on less. She had a way of passing her two arms about Rantoul's great one and clinging to him in a weak, dependent way that was quite charming.

When Cyrus Glover was informed that his daughter intended to marry a dauber in paints, he started for Paris on ten hours' notice. But Mrs. Glover who was just as resolved on social conquests as Glover was in controlling the plate-glass field, went down to meet him at the boat, and by the time the train entered the St. Lazare Station, he had been completely disciplined and brought to understand that a painter was one thing and that a Rantoul, who happened to paint, was quite another. When he had known Rantoul a week; and listened open-mouthed to his eloquent schemes for reordering the universe, and the arts in particular, he was willing to swear that he was one of the geniuses of the world.

The wedding took place shortly, and Cyrus Glover gave the bridegroom a check for $100,000, "so that he wouldn't have to be bothering his wife for pocket-money." Herkimer was the best man, and the Quarter attended in force, with much outward enthusiasm. The bride and groom departed for a two-year's trip around the world, that Rantoul might inspire himself with the treasures of Italy, Greece, India, and Japan.

Every one, even Herkimer, agreed that Rantoul was the luckiest man in Paris; that he had found just the wife who was suited to him, whose fortune would open every opportunity for his genius to develop.

"In the first place," said Bennett, when the group had returned to Herkimer's studio to continue the celebration, "let me remark that in general I don't approve of marriage for an artist."

"Nor I," cried Chatterton, and the chorus answered, "Nor I."

"I shall never marry," continued Bennett.

"Never," cried Chatterton, who beat a tattoo on the piano with his heel to accompany the chorus of assent.

"But - I add but - in this case my opinion is that Rantoul has found a pure diamond."

"True!"

"In the first place, she knows nothing at all about art, which is an enormous advantage."

"Bravo!"

"In the second place, she knows nothing about anything else, which is better still."

"Cynic! You hate clever women," cried Jacobus.

"There's a reason."

"All the same, Bennett's right. The wife of an artist should be a creature of impulses and not ideas."

"True."

"In the third place," continued Bennett, "she believes Rantoul is a demigod. Everything he will do will be the most wonderful thing in the world, and to have a little person you are madly in love with think that is enormous."

"All of which is not very complimentary to the bride," said Herkimer.

"Find me one like her," cried Bennett.

"Ditto," said Chatterton and Jacobus with enthusiasm.

"There is only one thing that worries me," said Bennett, seriously. "Isn't there too much money?"

"Not for Rantoul."

"He's a rebel."

"You'll see; he'll stir up the world with it."

Herkimer himself had approved of the marriage in a whole-hearted way. The childlike ways of Tina Glover had convinced him, and as he was concerned only with the future of his friend, he agreed with the rest that nothing luckier could have happened.

Three years passed, during which he received occasional letters from his old chum, not quite so spontaneous as he had expected, but filled with the wonder of the ancient worlds. Then the intervals became longer, and longer, and finally no letters came.

He learned in a vague way that the Rantouls had settled in the East somewhere near New York, but he waited in vain for the news of the stir in the world of art that Rantoul's first exhibitions should produce.

His friends who visited in America returned without

news of Rantoul; there was a rumor that he had gone with his father-in-law into the organization of some new railroad or trust. But even this report was vague, and as he could not understand what could have happened, it remained for a long time to him a mystery. Then he forgot it.

Ten years after Rantoul's marriage to little Tina Glover, Herkimer returned to America. The last years had placed him in the foreground of the sculptors of the world. He had that strangely excited consciousness that he was a figure in the public eye. Reporters rushed to meet him on his arrival, societies organized dinners to him, magazines sought the details of his life's struggle. Withal, however, he felt a strange loneliness, and an aloofness from the clamoring world about him. He remembered the old friendship in the starlit garret of the Rue de l'Ombre, and, learning Rantoul's address, wrote him. Three days later he received the following answer:

> *Dear Old Boy:*
>
> I'm delighted to find that you have remembered me in your fame. Run up this Saturday for a week at least. I'll show you some fine scenery, and we'll recall the days of the Cafe des Lilacs together. My wife sends her greetings also.
>
> Clyde.

This letter made Herkimer wonder. There was nothing on which he could lay his finger, and yet there was something that was not there. With some misgivings he packed his bag and took the train, calling up again to his mind the picture of Rantoul, with his shabby trousers pulled up, decorating his ankles with lavender and black, roaring all the while with his rumbling laughter.

At the station only the chauffeur was down to meet him. A correct footman, moving on springs, took his bag, placed him in the back seat, and spread a duster for him. They turned through a pillared gateway, Renaissance style, passed a gardener's lodge, with hothouses flashing in the reclining sun, and fled noiselessly along the macadam road that twined through a formal grove. All at once they were before the house, red brick and marble, with wide-flung porte-cochere and verandas, beyond which could be seen immaculate lawns, and in the middle distances the sluggish gray of a river that crawled down from the turbulent hills on the horizon. Another creature in livery tripped down the steps and held the door for him. He passed perplexed into the hall, which was fresh with the breeze that swept through open French windows.

"Mr. Herkimer, isn't it?"

He turned to find a woman of mannered assurance holding out her hand correctly to him, and under the panama that topped the pleasant effect of her white polo-coat he looked into the eyes of that Tina Glover, who once had caught his rough hand in her little ones and said timidly:

"You'll always be my friend, my best, just as you are Clyde's, won't you? And I may call you Britt or Old Boy or Old Top, just as Clyde does?"

He looked at her amazed. She was prettier, undeniably

so. She had learned the art of being a woman, and she gave him her hand as though she had granted a favor.

"Yes," he said shortly, freezing all at once. "Where's Clyde?"

"He had to play in a polo-match. He's just home taking a tub," she said easily. "Will you go to your room first? I didn't ask any one in for dinner. I supposed you would rather chat together of old times. You have become a tremendous celebrity, haven't you? Clyde is so proud of you."

"I'll go to my room now," he said shortly.

The valet had preceded him, opening his valise and smoothing out his evening clothes on the lace bedspread.

"I'll attend to that," he said curtly. "You may go."

He stood at the window, in the long evening hour of the June day, frowning to himself. "By George! I've a mind to clear out," he said, thoroughly angry.

At this moment there came a vigorous rap, and Rantoul in slippers and lilac dressing-gown broke in, with hair still wet from his shower.

"The same as ever, bless the Old Top!" he cried, catching him up in one of the old-time bear-hugs. "I say, don't think me inhospitable. Had to play a confounded match. We beat 'em, too; lost six pounds doing it, though. Jove! but you look natural! I say, that was a stunning thing you did for Philadelphia - the audacity of it. How do you like my place? I've got four children, too. What do you think of that? Nothing finer. Well, tell me what you're doing."

Herkimer relented before the familiar rush of enthusiasm and questions, and the conversation began on a natural footing. He looked at Rantoul, aware of the social change that had taken place in him. The old aggressiveness, the look of the wolf, had gone; about him was an enthusiastic urbanity. He seemed clean cut, virile, overflowing with vitality, only it was a different vitality, the snap and decision of a man-of-affairs, not the untamed outrush of the artist.

They had spoken scarcely a short five minutes when a knock came on the door and a footman's voice said:

"Mrs. Rantoul wishes you not to be late for dinner, sir."

"Very well, very well," said Rantoul, with a little impatience. "I always forget the time. Jove! it's good to see you again; you'll give us a week at least. Meet you downstairs."

When Herkimer had dressed and descended, his host and hostess were still up-stairs. He moved through the rooms, curiously noting the contents of the walls. There were several paintings of value, a series of drawings by Boucher, a replica or two of his own work; but he sought without success for something from the brush of Clyde Rantoul. At dinner he was aware of a sudden uneasiness. Mrs. Rantoul, with the flattering smile that recalled Tina Glover, pressed him with innumerable questions, which he answered with constraint, always aware of the dull simulation of interest in her eyes.

Twice during the meal Rantoul was called to the telephone for a conversation at long distance.

"Clyde is becoming quite a power in Wall Street," said Mrs. Rantoul, with an approving smile. "Father says he's the strength of the younger men. He has really a genius for organization."

"It's a wonderful time, Britt," said Rantoul, resuming his place. "There's nothing like it anywhere on the face of the globe - the possibilities of concentration and simplification here in business. It's a great game, too, matching your wits against another's. We're building empires of trade, order out of chaos. I'm making an awful lot of money."

Herkimer remained obstinately silent during the rest of the dinner. Everything seemed to fetter him - the constraint of dining before the silent, flitting butler, servants who whisked his plate away before he knew it, the succession of unrecognizable dishes, the constant jargon of social eavesdroppings that Mrs. Rantoul pressed into action the moment her husband's recollections exiled her from the conversation; but above all, the indefinable enmity that seemed to well out from his hostess, and which he seemed to divine occasionally when the ready smile left her lips and she was forced to listen to things she did not understand.

When they rose from the table, Rantoul passed his arm about his wife and said something in her ear, at which she smiled and patted his hand.

"I am very proud of my husband, Mr. Herkimer," she said with a little bob of her head in which was a sense of proprietorship. "You'll see."

"Suppose we stroll out for a little smoke in the garden," said Rantoul.

"What, you're going to leave me?" she said instantly, with a shade of vague uneasiness, that Herkimer perceived.

"We sha'n't be long, dear," said Rantoul, pinching her ear. "Our chatter won't interest you. Send the coffee out into the rose cupola."

They passed out into the open porch, but Herkimer was aware of the little woman standing irresolutely tapping with her thin finger on the table, and he said to himself: "She's a little ogress of jealousy. What the deuce is she afraid I'll say to him?"

They rambled through sweet-scented paths, under the high-flung network of stars, hearing only the crunching of little pebbles under foot.

"You've given up painting?" said Herkimer all at once.

"Yes, though that doesn't count," said Rantoul, abruptly; but there was in his voice a different note, something of the restlessness of the old Don Furioso. "Talk to me of the Quarter. Who's at the Cafe des Lilacs now? They tell me that little Ragin we used to torment so has made some great decorations. What became of that pretty girl in the creamery of the Rue de l'Ombre who used to help us over the lean days?"

"Whom you christened Our Lady of the Sparrows?" "Yes, yes. You know I sent her the silk dress and the earrings I promised her."

Herkimer began to speak of one thing and another, of Bennett, who had gone dramatically to the Transvaal; of Le Gage, who was now in the forefront of the younger group of landscapists; of the old types that still came faithfully to the Cafe des Lilacs, - the old chess-players, the fat proprietor, with his fat wife and three fat children who dined there regularly every Sunday, - of the new revolutionary ideas among the younger men that were beginning to assert themselves.

"Let's sit down," said Rantoul, as though suffocating.

They placed themselves in wicker easy-chairs, under the heavy-scented rose cupola, disdaining the coffee that waited on a table. From where they were a red-tiled walk, with flower beds nodding in enchanted sleep, ran to the veranda. The porch windows were open, and in the golden lamplight Herkimer saw the figure of Tina Glover bent intently over an embroidery, drawing her needle with uneven stitches, her head seeming inclined to catch the faintest sound. The waiting, nervous pose, the slender figure on guard, brought to him a strange, almost uncanny sensation of mystery, and feeling the sudden change in the mood of the man at his side, he gazed at the figure of the wife and said to himself:

"I'd give a good deal to know what's passing through that little head. What is she afraid of?"

"You're surprised to find me as I am," said Rantoul, abruptly breaking the silence.

"Yes."

"You can't understand it?"

"When did you give up painting?" said Herkimer, shortly, with a sure feeling that the hour of confidences had come.

"Seven years ago."

"Why in God's name did you do it?" said Herkimer, flinging away his cigar angrily. "You weren't just any one - Tom, Dick, or Harry. You had something to say, man. Listen. I know what I'm talking about, - I've seen the whole procession in the last ten years, - you were one in a thousand. You were a creator. You had ideas; you were meant to be a leader, to head a movement. You had more downright savage power, undeveloped, but tugging at the chain, than any man I've known. Why did you do it?"

"I had almost forgotten," said Rantoul, slowly. "Are you sure?"

"Am I sure?" said Herkimer, furiously. "I say what I mean; you know it."

"Yes, that's true," said Rantoul. He stretched out his hand and drank his coffee, but without knowing what he did. "Well, that's all of the past - what might have been."

"But why?"

"Britt, old fellow," said Rantoul at last, speaking as though to himself, "did you ever have a moment when you suddenly got out of yourself, looked at yourself and at your life as a spectator? - saw the strange strings that had pulled you this way and that, and realized what might have been had you turned one corner at a certain day of your life instead of another?"

"No, I've gone where I wanted to go," said Herkimer, obstinately.

"You think so. Well, to-night I can see myself for the first time," said Rantoul. Then he added meditatively, "I have done not one single thing I wanted to."

"But why - why?"

"You have brought it all back to me," said Rantoul, ignoring this question. "It hurts. I suppose to-morrow I shall resent it, but to-night I feel too deeply. There is nothing free about us in this world, Britt. I profoundly believe that. Everything we do from morning to night is dictated by the direction of those about us. An enemy, some one in the open, we can combat and resist; but it is those that are nearest to us who disarm us because they love us, that change us most, that thwart our desires, and make over our lives. Nothing in this world is so inexorable, so terribly, terribly irresistible as a woman without strength, without logic, without vision, who only loves."

"He is going to say things he will regret," thought Herkimer, and yet he did not object. Instead, he glanced down the dimly flushed path to the house where Mrs. Rantoul was sitting, her embroidery on her lap, her head raised as though listening. Suddenly he said:

"Look here, Clyde, do you want to tell me this?"

"Yes, I do; it's life. Why not? We are at the age when we've got to face things."

"Still - "

"Let me go on," said Rantoul, stopping him. He reached out absent-mindedly, and drank the second cup. "Let me say now, Britt, for fear you'll misunderstand, there has never been the slightest quarrel between my wife and me. She loves me absolutely; nothing else in this world exists for her. It has always been so; she cannot bear even to have me out of her sight. I am very happy. Only there is in such a love something of the tiger - a fierce animal jealousy of every one and everything which could even for a moment take my thoughts away. At this moment she is probably suffering untold pangs because she thinks I am regretting the days in which she was not in my life."

"And because she could not understand your art, she hated it," said Herkimer, with a growing anger.

"No, it wasn't that. It was something more subtle, more instinctive, more impossible to combat," said Rantoul, shaking his head. "Do you know what is the great essential to the artist - to whoever creates? The sense of privacy, the power to isolate his own genius from everything in the world, to be absolutely concentrated. To create we must be alone, have strange, unuttered thoughts, just as in the realms of the soul every human being must have moments of complete isolation - thoughts, reveries, moods, that cannot be shared with even those we love best. You don't understand that."

"Yes, I do."

"At the bottom we human beings come and depart absolutely alone. Friendship, love, all that we

Owen Johnson

instinctively seek to rid ourselves of, this awful solitude of the soul, avail nothing. Well, what others shrink from, the artist must seek."

"But you could not make her understand that?"

"I was dealing with a child," said Rantoul. "I loved that child, and I could not bear even to see a frown of unhappiness cloud her face. Then she adored me. What can be answered to that?"

"That's true."

"At first it was not so difficult. We passed around the world - Greece, India, Japan. She came and sat by my side when I took my easel; every stroke of my brush seemed like a miracle. A hundred times she would cry out her delight. Naturally that amused me. From time to time I would suspend the sittings and reward my patient little audience - "

"And the sketches?"

"They were not what I wanted," said Rantoul with a little laugh; "but they were not bad. When I returned here and opened my studio, it began to be difficult. She could not understand that I wanted to work eighteen hours a day. She begged for my afternoons. I gave in. She embraced me frantically and said; 'Oh, how good you are! Now I won't be jealous any more, and every morning I will come with you and inspire you.'"

"Every morning," said Herkimer, softly.

"Yes," said Rantoul, with a little hesitation, "every morning. She fluttered about the studio like a pink-and-white butterfly, sending me a kiss from her dainty fingers whenever I looked her way. She watched over my shoulder every stroke, and when I did something that pleased her, I felt her lips on my neck, behind my ear, and heard her say, 'That is your reward.'"

"Every day?" said Herkimer.

"Every day."

"And when you had a model?"

"Oh, then it was worse. She treated the models as though they were convicts, watching them out of the corners of her eyes. Her demonstration of affection redoubled, her caresses never stopped, as though she wished to impress upon them her proprietorship. Those days she was really jealous."

"God - how could you stand it?" said Herkimer, violently.

"To be frank, the more she outraged me as an artist, the more she pleased me as a man. To be loved so absolutely, especially if you are sensitive to such things, has an intoxication of its own, yes, she fascinated me more and more."

"Extraordinary."

"One day I tried to make her understand that I had need to be alone. She listened to me solemnly, with only a little quiver of her lips, and let me go. When I returned, I found her eyes swollen with weeping and her heart bursting."

"And you took her in your arms and promised never to send her away again."

"Naturally. Then I began to go out into society to please her. Next something very interesting came up, and I neglected my studio for a morning. The same thing happened again and again. I had a period of wild revolt, of bitter anger, in which I resolved to be firm, to insist on my privacy, to make the fight."

"And you never did?"

"When her arms were about me, when I saw her eyes, full of adoration and passion, raised to my own, I forgot all my irritation in my happiness as a man. I said to myself, 'Life is short; it is better to be loved than to wait for glory.' One afternoon, under the pretext of examining the grove, I stole away to the studio, and pulled out some of the old things that I had done in Paris - and sat and gazed at them. My throat began to fill, and I felt the tears coming to my eyes, when I looked around and saw her standing wide-eyed at the door.

"'What are you doing?' she said.

"'Looking at some of the old things.'

"'You regret those days?'

"'Of course not.'

"'Then why do you steal away from me, make a pretext to come here? Isn't my love great enough for you? Do you want to put me out of your life altogether? You used to tell me that I inspired you. If you want, we'll give up the afternoons. I'll come here, I'll be your model, I'll sit for you by the hour - only don't shut the door on me!'

"She began to cry. I took her in my arms, said everything that she wished me to say, heedlessly, brutally, not caring what I said.

"That night I ran off, resolved to end it all - to save what I longed for. I remained five hours trudging in the night - pulled back and forth. I remembered my children. I came back, - told a lie. The next day I shut the door of the studio not on her, but on myself.

"For months I did nothing. I was miserable. She saw it at last, and said to me:

"'You ought to work. You aren't happy doing nothing. I've arranged something for you.'

"I raised my head in amazement, as she continued, clapping her hands with delight:

"'I've talked it all over with papa. You'll go into his office. You'll do big things. He's quite enthusiastic, and I promised for you.'

"I went. I became interested. I stayed. Now I am like any other man, domesticated, conservative, living my life, and she has not the slightest idea of what she has killed."

"Let us go in," said Herkimer, rising.

"And you say I could have left a name?" said Rantoul, bitterly.

"You were wrong to tell me all this," said Herkimer.

"I owed you the explanation. What could I do?"

"Lie."

"Why?"

"Because, after such a confidence, it is impossible for you ever to see me again. You know it."

"Nonsense. I - "

"Let's go back."

Full of dull anger and revolt, Herkimer led the way. Rantoul, after a few steps, caught him by the sleeve.

"Don't take it too seriously, Britt. I don't revolt any more. I'm no longer the Rantoul you knew."

"That's just the trouble," said Herkimer, cruelly.

When their steps sounded near, Mrs. Rantoul rose hastily, spilling her silk and needles on the floor. She gave her husband a swift, searching look, and said with her flattering smile:

"Mr. Herkimer, you must be a very interesting talker. I am quite jealous."

"I am rather tired," he answered, bowing. "If you'll excuse me, I'll go off to bed."

"Really?" she said, raising her eyes. She extended her hand, and he took it with almost the physical repulsion with which one would touch the hand of a criminal. The next morning he left.

Owen Johnson

III

When Herkimer had finished, he shrugged his shoulders, gave a short laugh, and, glancing at the clock, went off in his curt, purposeful manner.

"Well, by Jove!" said Steingall, recovering first from the spell of the story, "doesn't that prove exactly what I said? They're jealous, they're all jealous, I tell you, jealous of everything you do. All they want us to do is to adore them. By Jove! Herkimer's right. Rantoul was the biggest of us all. She murdered him just as much as though she had put a knife in him."

"She did it on purpose," said De Gollyer. "There was nothing childlike about her, either. On the contrary, I consider her a clever, a devilishly clever woman."

"Of course she did. They're all clever, damn them!" said Steingall, explosively. "Now, what do you say, Quinny? I say that an artist who marries might just as well tie a rope around his neck and present it to his wife and have it over."

"On the contrary," said Quinny, with a sudden inspiration reorganizing his whole battle front, "every artist should marry. The only danger is that he may marry happily."

"What?" cried Steingall. "But you said - "

"My dear boy, I have germinated some new ideas," said Quinny, unconcerned. "The story has a moral, - I detest morals, - but this has one. An artist should always marry unhappily, and do you know why? Purely a question of chemistry. Towsey, when do you work the best?"

"How do you mean?" said Towsey, rousing himself.

"I've heard you say that you worked best when your nerves were all on edge - night out, cucumbers, thunder-storm, or a touch of fever."

"Yes, that's so."

"Can any one work well when everything is calm?" continued Quinny, triumphantly, to the amazement of Rankin and Steingall. "Can you work on a clear spring day, when nothing bothers you and the first of the month is two weeks off, eh? Of course you can't. Happiness is the enemy of the artist. It puts to sleep the faculties. Contentment is a drug. My dear men, an artist should always be unhappy. Perpetual state of fermentation sets the nerves throbbing, sensitive to impressions. Exaltation and remorse, anger and inspiration, all hodge-podge, chemical action and reaction, all this we are blessed with when we are unhappily married. Domestic infelicity drives us to our art; happiness makes us neglect it. Shall I tell you what I do when everything is smooth, no nerves, no inspiration, fat, puffy Sunday-dinner-feeling, too happy, can't work? I go home and start a quarrel with my wife."

Owen Johnson

"And then you *can* work," cried Steingall, roaring with laughter. "By Jove, you *are* immense!"

"Never better," said Quinny, who appeared like a prophet.

The four artists, who had listened to Herkimer's story in that gradual thickening depression which the subject of matrimony always let down over them, suddenly brightened visibly. On their faces appeared the look of inward speculation, and then a ray of light.

Little Towsey, who from his arrival had sulked, fretted, and fumed, jumped up energetically and flung away his third cigar.

"Here, where are you going?" said Rankin in protest.

"Over to the studio," said Towsey, quite unconsciously. "I feel like a little work."

ONE HUNDRED IN THE DARK

They were discussing languidly, as such groups do, seeking from each topic a peg on which to hang a few epigrams that might be retold in the lip currency of the club - Steingall, the painter, florid of gesture and effete, foreign in type, with black-rimmed glasses and trailing ribbon of black silk that cut across his cropped beard and cavalry mustaches; De Gollyer, a critic, who preferred to be known as a man about town, short, feverish, incisive, who slew platitudes with one adjective and tagged a reputation with three; Rankin, the architect, always in a defensive explanatory attitude, who held his elbows on the table, his hands before his long sliding nose, and gestured with his fingers; Quinny, the illustrator, long and gaunt, with a predatory eloquence that charged irresistibly down on any subject, cut it off, surrounded it, and raked it with enfilading wit and satire; and Peters, whose methods of existence were a mystery, a young man of fifty, who had done nothing and who knew every one by his first name, the club postman, who carried the tittle-tattle, the *bon mots* and the news of the day, who drew up a petition a week and pursued the house committee with a daily grievance.

About the latticed porch, which ran around the sanded yard with its feeble fountain and futile evergreens, other groups were eying one another, or engaging in desultory conversation, oppressed with the heaviness of the night.

At the round table, Quinny alone, absorbing energy as he devoured the conversation, having routed Steingall on the Germans and archaeology and Rankin on the origins of the Lord's Prayer, had seized a chance remark of De Gollyer's to say:

"There are only half a dozen stories in the world. Like everything that's true it isn't true." He waved his long, gouty fingers in the direction of Steingall, who, having been silenced, was regarding him with a look of sleepy indifference. "What is more to the point, is the small number of human relations that are so simple and yet so fundamental that they can be eternally played upon, redressed, and reinterpreted in every language, in every age, and yet remain inexhaustible in the possibility of variations."

"By George, that is so," said Steingall, waking up. "Every art does go back to three or four notes. In composition it is the same thing. Nothing new - nothing new since a thousand years. By George, that is true! We invent nothing, nothing!"

"Take the eternal triangle," said Quinny hurriedly, not to surrender his advantage, while Rankin and De Gollyer in a bored way continued to gaze dreamily at a vagrant star or two. "Two men and a woman, or two women and a man. Obviously it should be classified as the first of the great original parent themes. Its variations extend into the thousands. By the way, Rankin, excellent opportunity, eh, for some of our modern, painstaking, unemployed jackasses to analyze and classify."

"Quite right," said Rankin without perceiving the satirical note. "Now there's De Maupassant's Fort comma la Mort - quite the most interesting variation - shows the turn a genius can give. There the triangle is the man of middle age, the mother he has loved in his youth and the daughter he comes to love. It forms, you might say, the head of a whole subdivision of modern continental literature."

"Quite wrong, Rankin, quite wrong," said Quinny, who would have stated the other side quite as imperiously. "What you cite is a variation of quite another theme, the Faust theme - old age longing for youth, the man who has loved longing for the love of his youth, which is youth itself. The triangle is the theme of jealousy, the most destructive and, therefore, the most dramatic of human passions. The Faust theme is the most fundamental and inevitable of all human experiences, the tragedy of life itself. Quite a different thing."

Rankin, who never agreed with Quinny unless Quinny maliciously took advantage of his prior announcement to agree with him, continued to combat this idea.

"You believe then," said De Gollyer after a certain moment had been consumed in hair splitting, "that the origin of all dramatic themes is simply the expression of some human emotion. In other words, there can exist no more parent themes than there are human emotions."

"I thank you, sir, very well put," said Quinny with a generous wave of his hand. "Why is the Three Musketeers a basic theme? Simply the interpretation of comradeship, the emotion one man feels for another, vital because it is the one peculiarly masculine emotion. Look at Du Maurier and Trilby, Kipling in Soldiers Three - simply the Three Musketeers."

"The Vie de Boheme?" suggested Steingall.

"In the real Vie de Boheme, yes," said Quinny viciously. "Not in the concocted sentimentalities that we now have served up to us by athletic tenors and consumptive elephants!"

Rankin, who had been silently deliberating on what had been left behind, now said cunningly and with evident purpose:

"All the same, I don't agree with you men at all. I believe there are situations, original situations, that are independent of your human emotions, that exist just because they are situations, accidental and nothing else."

"As for instance?" said Quinny, preparing to attack.

"Well, I'll just cite an ordinary one that happens to come to my mind," said Rankin, who had carefully selected his test. "In a group of seven or eight, such as we are here, a theft takes place; one man is the thief - which one? I'd like to know what emotion that interprets, and yet it certainly is an original theme, at the bottom of a whole literature."

This challenge was like a bomb.

"Not the same thing."

"Detective stories, bah!"

"Oh, I say, Rankin, that's literary melodrama."

Rankin, satisfied, smiled and winked victoriously over to Tommers, who was listening from an adjacent table.

"Of course your suggestion is out of order, my dear man, to this extent," said Quinny, who never surrendered, "in that I am talking of fundamentals and you are citing details. Nevertheless, I could answer that the situation you give, as well as the whole school it belongs to, can be traced back to the commonest of human emotions, curiosity; and that the story of Bluebeard and the Moonstone are to all purposes identically the same."

At this Steingall, who had waited hopefully, gasped and made as though to leave the table.

"I shall take up your contention," said Quinny without pause for breath, "first, because you have opened up one of my pet topics, and, second, because it gives me a chance to talk." He gave a sidelong glance at Steingall and winked at De Gollyer. "What is the peculiar fascination that the detective problem exercises over the human mind? You will say curiosity. Yes and no. Admit at once that the whole art of a detective story consists in the statement of the problem. Any one can do it. I can do it. Steingall even can do it. The solution doesn't count. It is usually banal; it should be prohibited. What interests us is, can we guess it? Just as an able-minded man will sit down for hours and fiddle over the puzzle column in a Sunday balderdash. Same idea. There you have it, the problem - the detective story. Now why the fascination? I'll tell you. It appeals to our curiosity, yes - but deeper to a sort of intellectual vanity. Here are six

Owen Johnson

matches, arrange them to make four squares; five men present, a theft takes place - who's the thief? Who will guess it first? Whose brain will show its superior cleverness - see? That's all - that's all there is to it."

"Out of all of which," said De Gollyer, "the interesting thing is that Rankin has supplied the reason why the supply of detective fiction is inexhaustible. It does all come down to the simplest terms. Seven possibilities, one answer. It is a formula, ludicrously simple, mechanical, and yet we will always pursue it to the end. The marvel is that writers should seek for any other formula when here is one so safe, that can never fail. By George, I could start up a factory on it."

"The reason is," said Rankin, "that the situation does constantly occur. It's a situation that any of us might get into any time. As a matter of fact, now, I personally know two such occasions when I was of the party; and devilish uncomfortable it was too."

"What happened?" said Steingall.

"Why, there is no story to it particularly. Once a mistake had been made and the other time the real thief was detected by accident a year later. In both cases only one or two of us knew what had happened."

De Gollyer had a similar incident to recall. Steingall, after reflection, related another that had happened to a friend.

"Of course, of course, my dear gentlemen," said Quinny impatiently, for he had been silent too long, "you are glorifying commonplaces. Every crime, I tell you, expresses itself in the terms of the picture puzzle that you feed to your six-year-old. It's only the variation that is interesting. Now quite the most remarkable turn of the complexities that can be developed is, of course, the well-known instance of the visitor at a club and the rare coin. Of course every one knows that? What?"

Rankin smiled in a bored, superior way, but the others protested their ignorance.

"Why, it's very well known," said Quinny lightly.

"A distinguished visitor is brought into a club - dozen men, say, present, at dinner, long table. Conversation finally veers around to curiosities and relics. One of the members present then takes from his pocket what he announces as one of the rarest coins in existence - passes it around the table. Coin travels back and forth, every one examining it, and the conversation goes to another topic, say the influence of the automobile on domestic infelicity, or some other such asininely intellectual club topic - you know? All at once the owner calls for his coin.

"The coin is nowhere to be found. Every one looks at every one else. First they suspect a joke. Then it becomes serious - the coin is immensely valuable. Who has taken it?

"The owner is a gentleman - does the gentlemanly idiotic thing of course, laughs, says he knows some one is playing a practical joke on him and that the coin will be returned to-morrow. The others refuse to leave the situation so. One man proposes that they all submit to a search. Every one gives his assent until it comes to the stranger. He refuses, curtly, roughly, without giving any reason. Uncomfortable silence - the man is a guest. No one knows him particularly well - but still he is a guest. One member tries to make him understand that no offense is offered, that the suggestion was simply to clear the atmosphere, and all that sort of bally rot, you know.

"'I refuse to allow my person to be searched,' says the stranger, very firm, very proud, very English, you know, 'and I refuse to give my reason for my action.'

"Another silence. The men eye him and then glance at one another. What's to be done? Nothing. There is etiquette - that magnificent inflated balloon. The visitor evidently has the coin - but he is their guest and etiquette protects him. Nice situation, eh?

"The table is cleared. A waiter removes a dish of fruit and there under the ledge of the plate where it had been pushed - is the coin. Banal explanation, eh? Of course. Solutions always should be. At once every one in profuse apologies! Whereupon the visitor rises and says:

"'Now I can give you the reason for my refusal to be searched. There are only two known specimens of the coin in existence, and the second happens to be here in my waistcoat pocket.'"

"Of course," said Quinny with a shrug of his shoulders, "the story is well invented, but the turn to it is very nice - very nice indeed."

"I did know the story," said Steingall, to be disagreeable; "the ending, though, is too obvious to be invented. The visitor should have had on him not another coin, but something absolutely different, something destructive, say, of a woman's reputation, and a great tragedy should have been threatened by the casual misplacing of the coin."

"I have heard the same story told in a dozen different ways," said Rankin.

"It has happened a hundred times. It must be continually happening," said Steingall.

"I know one extraordinary instance," said Peters, who up to the present, secure in his climax, had waited with a professional smile until the big guns had been silenced. "In fact, the most extraordinary instance of this sort I have ever heard."

"Peters, you little rascal," said Quinny with a sidelong glance, "I perceive you have quietly been letting us dress the stage for you."

"It is not a story that will please every one," said Peters, to whet their appetite.

"Why not?"

"Because you will want to know what no one can ever know."

"It has no conclusion then?"

"Yes and no. As far as it concerns a woman, quite the most remarkable woman I have ever met, the story is complete. As for the rest, it is what it is, because it is one example where literature can do nothing better than record."

"Do I know the woman?" asked De Gollyer, who flattered himself on passing through every class of society.

"Possibly, but no more than any one else."

"An actress?"

"What she has been in the past I don't know - a promoter would better describe her. Undoubtedly she has been behind the scenes in many an untold intrigue of the business world. A very feminine woman, and yet, as you shall see, with an unusual instantaneous masculine power of decision."

"Peters," said Quinny, waving a warning finger, "you are destroying your story. Your preface will bring an anticlimax."

"You shall judge," said Peters, who waited until his audience was in strained attention before opening his story. "The names are, of course, disguises."

Mrs. Rita Kildair inhabited a charming bachelor-girl studio, very elegant, of the duplex pattern, in one of the buildings just off Central Park West. She knew pretty nearly every one in that indescribable society in New York that is drawn from all levels, and that imposes but one condition for membership - to be amusing. She knew every one and no one knew her. No one knew beyond the vaguest rumors her history or her means. No one had ever heard of a Mr. Kildair. There was always about her a certain defensive reserve the moment the limits of acquaintanceship had been reached. She had a certain amount of money, she knew a certain number of men in Wall Street affairs and her studio was furnished with taste and even distinction. She was of any age. She might have suffered everything or nothing at all. In this mingled society her invitations were eagerly sought, her dinners were spontaneous, and the discussions, though gay and usually daring, were invariably under the control of wit and good taste.

On the Sunday night of this adventure she had, according to her invariable custom, sent away her Japanese butler and invited to an informal chafing-dish supper seven of her more congenial friends, all of whom, as much as could be said of any one, were habitues of the studio.

At seven o'clock, having finished dressing, she put in order her bedroom, which formed a sort of free passage between the studio and a small dining room to the kitchen beyond. Then, going into the studio, she lit a wax taper and was in the act of touching off the brass candlesticks that lighted the room when three knocks sounded on the door and a Mr. Flanders, a broker, compact, nervously alive, well groomed, entered with the informality of assured acquaintance.

"You are early," said Mrs. Kildair, in surprise.

"On the contrary, you are late," said the broker, glancing at his watch.

"Then be a good boy and help me with the candles," she said, giving him a smile and a quick pressure of her fingers.

He obeyed, asking nonchalantly:

Owen Johnson

"I say, dear lady, who's to be here to-night?"

"The Enos Jacksons."

"I thought they were separated."

"Not yet."

"Very interesting! Only you, dear lady, would have thought of serving us a couple on the verge."

"It's interesting, isn't it?"

"Assuredly. Where did you know Jackson?"

"Through the Warings. Jackson's a rather doubtful person, isn't he?"

"Let's call him a very sharp lawyer," said Flanders defensively. "They tell me, though, he is on the wrong side of the market - in deep."

"And you?"

"Oh, I? I'm a bachelor," he said with a shrug of his shoulders, "and if I come a cropper it makes no difference."

"Is that possible?" she said, looking at him quickly.

"Probable even. And who else is coming?"

"Maude Lille - you know her?"

"I think not."

"You met her here - a journalist."

"Quite so, a strange career."

"Mr. Harris, a clubman, is coming, and the Stanley Cheevers."

"The Stanley Cheevers!" said Flanders with some surprise. "Are we going to gamble?"

"You believe in that scandal about bridge?"

"Certainly not," said Flanders, smiling. "You see I was present. The Cheevers play a good game, a well united game, and have an unusual system of makes. By-the-way, it's Jackson who is very attentive to Mrs. Cheever, isn't it?"

"Quite right."

"What a charming party," said Flanders flippantly. "And where does Maude Lille come in?"

"Don't joke. She is in a desperate way," said Mrs. Kildair, with a little sadness in her eyes.

"And Harris?"

"Oh, he is to make the salad and cream the chicken."

"Ah, I see the whole party. I, of course, am to add the element of respectability."

"Of what?"

She looked at him steadily until he turned away ,

dropping his glance.

"Don't be an ass with me, my dear Flanders."

"By George, if this were Europe I'd wager you were in the secret service, Mrs. Kildair."

"Thank you."

She smiled appreciatively and moved about the studio, giving the finishing touches. The Stanley Cheevers entered, a short fat man with a vacant fat face and a slow-moving eye, and his wife, voluble, nervous, overdressed and pretty. Mr. Harris came with Maude Lille, a woman, straight, dark, Indian, with great masses of somber hair held in a little too loosely for neatness, with thick, quick lips and eyes that rolled away from the person who was talking to her. The Enos Jacksons were late and still agitated as they entered. His forehead had not quite banished the scowl, nor her eyes the scorn. He was of the type that never lost his temper, but caused others to lose theirs, immovable in his opinions, with a prowling walk, a studied antagonism in his manner, and an impudent look that fastened itself unerringly on the weakness in the person to whom he spoke. Mrs. Jackson, who seemed fastened to her husband by an invisible leash, had a hunted, resisting quality back of a certain desperate dash, which she assumed rather than felt in her attitude toward life. One looked at her curiously and wondered what such a nature would do in a crisis, with a lurking sense of a woman who carried with her her own impending tragedy.

As soon as the company had been completed and the incongruity of the selection had been perceived, a smile of malicious anticipation ran the rounds, which the hostess cut short by saying:

"Well, now that every one is here, this is the order of the night: You can quarrel all you want, you can whisper all the gossip you can think of about one another, but every one is to be amusing! Also every one is to help with the dinner - nothing formal and nothing serious. We may all be bankrupt to-morrow, divorced or dead, but to-night we will be gay - that is the invariable rule of the house!"

Immediately a nervous laughter broke out and the company chattering began to scatter through the rooms.

Mrs. Kildair, stopping in her bedroom, donned a Watteaulike cooking apron, and slipping her rings from her fingers fixed the three on her pincushion with a hatpin.

"Your rings are beautiful, dear, beautiful," said the low voice of Maude Lille, who with Harris and Mrs. Cheever were in the room.

"There's only one that is very valuable," said Mrs. Kildair, touching with her thin fingers the ring that lay uppermost, two large diamonds, flanking a magnificent sapphire.

"It is beautiful - very beautiful," said the journalist, her eyes fastened to it with an uncontrollable fascination. She put out her fingers and let them rest caressingly on the sapphire, withdrawing them quickly as though the contact had burned them.

"It must be very valuable," she said, her breath catching a little. Mrs. Cheever, moving forward, suddenly looked at the ring.

"It cost five thousand six years ago," said Mrs. Kildair, glancing down at it. "It has been my talisman ever since. For the moment, however, I am cook; Maude Lille, you are scullery maid; Harris is the chef, and we are under his orders. Mrs. Cheever, did you ever peel onions?"

"Good Heavens, no!" said Mrs. Cheever, recoiling.

"Well, there are no onions to peel," said Mrs. Kildair, laughing. "All you'll have to do is to help set the table. On to the kitchen!"

Under their hostess's gay guidance the seven guests began to circulate busily through the rooms, laying the table, grouping the chairs, opening bottles, and preparing the material for the chafing dishes. Mrs. Kildair in the kitchen ransacked the ice box, and with her own hands chopped the *fines herbes*, shredded the chicken and measured the cream.

"Flanders, carry this in carefully," she said, her hands in a towel. "Cheever, stop watching your wife and put the salad bowl on the table. Everything ready, Harris? All right. Every one sit down. I'll be right in."

She went into her bedroom, and divesting herself of her apron hung it in the closet. Then going to her dressing table she drew the hatpin from the pincushion and carelessly slipped the rings on her fingers. All at once she frowned and looked quickly at her hand. Only two rings were there, the third ring, the one with the sapphire and the two diamonds, was missing.

"Stupid," she said to herself, and returned to her dressing table. All at once she stopped. She remembered quite clearly putting the pin through the three rings.

She made no attempt to search further, but remained without moving, her fingers drumming slowly on the table, her head to one side, her lip drawn in a little between her teeth, listening with a frown to the babble from the outer room. Who had taken the ring? Each of her guests had had a dozen opportunities in the course of the time she had been busy in the kitchen.

"Too much time before the mirror, dear lady," called out Flanders gaily, who from where he was seated could see her.

"It is not he," she said quickly. Then she reconsidered. "Why not? He is clever - who knows? Let me think."

To gain time she walked back slowly into the kitchen, her head bowed, her thumb between her teeth.

"Who has taken it?"

She ran over the character of her guests and their situations as she knew them. Strangely enough, at each her mind stopped upon some reason that might explain a sudden temptation.

"I shall find out nothing this way," she said to herself after a moment's deliberation; "that is not the important thing to me just now. The important thing is to get the ring back."

And slowly, deliberately, she began to walk back and forth, her clenched hand beating the deliberate rhythmic measure of her journey.

Five minutes later, as Harris, installed *en maitre* over the chafing dish, was giving directions, spoon in the air, Mrs. Kildair came into the room like a lengthening shadow. Her entrance had been made with scarcely a perceptible sound, and yet each guest was aware of it at the same moment, with a little nervous start.

"Heavens, dear lady," exclaimed Flanders, "you come in on us like a Greek tragedy! What is it you have for us, a surprise?"

As he spoke she turned her swift glance on him, drawing her forehead together until the eyebrows ran in a straight line.

"I have something to say to you," she said in a sharp, businesslike manner, watching the company with penetrating eagerness.

There was no mistaking the seriousness of her voice. Mr. Harris extinguished the oil lamp, covering the chafing dish clumsily with a discordant, disagreeable sound. Mrs. Cheever and Mrs. Enos Jackson swung about abruptly, Maude Lille rose a little from her seat, while the men imitated these movements of expectancy with a clumsy shuffling of the feet.

"Mr. Enos Jackson?"

"Yes, Mrs. Kildair."

"Kindly do as I ask you."

"Certainly."

She had spoken his name with a peremptory positiveness that was almost an accusation. He rose calmly, raising his eyebrows a little in surprise.

"Go to the door," she continued, shifting her glance from him to the others. "Are you there? Lock it. Bring me the key."

He executed the order without bungling, and returning stood before her, tendering the key.

"You've locked it?" she said, making the words an excuse to bury her glance in his.

"As you wished me to."

"Thanks."

She took from him the key and, shifting slightly, likewise locked the door into her bedroom through which she had come.

Then transferring the keys to her left hand, seemingly unaware of Jackson, who still awaited her further commands, her eyes studied a moment the possibilities of the apartment.

"Mr. Cheever?" she said in a low voice.

"Yes, Mrs. Kildair."

"Blow out all the candles except the candelabrum on the table."

"Put out the lights, Mrs. Kildair?"

"At once."

Mr. Cheever, in rising, met the glance of his wife, and the look of questioning and wonder that passed did not escape the hostess.

"But, my dear Mrs. Kildair," said Mrs. Jackson with a little nervous catch of her breath, "what is it? I'm getting terribly worked up! My nerves - "

"Miss Lille?" said the voice of command.

"Yes."

The journalist, calmer than the rest, had watched the proceedings without surprise, as though forewarned by professional instinct that something of importance was about to take place. Now she rose quietly with an almost stealthy motion.

"Put the candelabrum on this table - here," said Mrs. Kildair, indicating a large round table on which a few books were grouped. "No, wait. Mr. Jackson, first clear off the table. I want nothing on it."

"But, Mrs. Kildair - " began Mrs. Jackson's shrill voice again.

"That's it. Now put down the candelabrum."

In a moment, as Mr. Cheever proceeded methodically on his errand, the brilliant crossfire of lights dropped in the studio, only a few smoldering wicks winking on the walls, while the high room seemed to grow more distant as it came under the sole dominion of the three candles bracketed in silver at the head of the bare mahogany table.

"Now listen!" said Mrs. Kildair, and her voice had in it a cold note. "My sapphire ring has just been stolen."

She said it suddenly, hurling the news among them and waiting ferret-like for some indications in the chorus that broke out.

"Stolen!"

"Oh, my dear Mrs. Kildair!"

"Stolen - by Jove!"

"You don't mean it!"

"What! Stolen here - to-night?"

"The ring has been taken within the last twenty minutes," continued Mrs. Kildair in the same determined, chiseled tone. "I am not going to mince words. The ring has been taken and the thief is among you."

For a moment nothing was heard but an indescribable gasp and a sudden turning and searching, then suddenly Cheever's deep bass broke out:

"Stolen! But, Mrs. Kildair, is it possible?"

"Exactly. There is not the slightest doubt," said Mrs. Kildair. "Three of you were in my bedroom when I placed my rings on the pincushion. Each of you has passed through there a dozen times since. My sapphire ring is gone, and one of you has taken it."

Mrs. Jackson gave a little scream, and reached heavily for a glass of water. Mrs. Cheever said something inarticulate in the outburst of masculine exclamation. Only Maude Lille's calm voice could be heard saying:

"Quite true. I was in the room when you took them off. The sapphire ring was on top."

"Now listen!" said Mrs. Kildair, her eyes on Maude Lille's eyes. "I am not going to mince words. I am not going to stand on ceremony. I'm going to have that ring back. Listen to me carefully. I'm going to have that ring back, and until I do, not a soul shall leave this room." She tapped on the table with her nervous knuckles. "Who has taken it I do not care to know. All I want is my ring. Now I'm going to make it possible for whoever took it to restore it without possibility of detection. The doors are locked and will stay locked. I am going to put out the lights, and I am going to count one hundred slowly. You will be in absolute darkness; no one will know or see what is done. But if at the end of that time the ring is not here on this table I shall telephone the police and have every one in this room searched. Am I quite clear?"

Suddenly she cut short the nervous outbreak of suggestions and in the same firm voice continued:

"Every one take his place about the table. That's it. That will do."

The women, with the exception of the inscrutable Maude Lille, gazed hysterically from face to face while the men, compressing their fingers, locking them or grasping their chins, looked straight ahead fixedly at their hostess.

Mrs. Kildair, havin calmly assured herself that all were ranged as she wished, blew out two of the three candles.

"I shall count one hundred, no more, no less," she said. "Either I get back that ring or every one in this room is to be searched, remember."

Leaning over, she blew out the remaining candle and snuffed it.

"One, two, three, four, five - "

She began to count with the inexorable regularity of a clock's ticking.

In the room every sound was distinct, the rustle of a dress, the grinding of a shoe, the deep, slightly asthmatic breathing of a man.

"Twenty, twenty-one, twenty-two, twenty-three - "

She continued to count, while in the methodic unvarying note of her voice there was a rasping reiteration that began to affect the company. A slight gasping breath, uncontrollable, almost on the verge of hysterics, was heard, and a man nervously clearing his throat.

"Forty-five, forty-six, forty-seven - "

Still nothing had happened. Mrs. Kildair did not vary her measure the slightest , only the sound became more metallic.

"Sixty-six, sixty-seven, sixty-eight, sixty-nine and seventy - "

Some one had sighed.

"Seventy-three, seventy-four, seventy-five, seventy-six, seventy-seven - "

All at once, clear, unmistakable, on the resounding plane of the table was heard a slight metallic note.

"The ring!"

It was Maude Lille's quick voice that had spoken. Mrs. Kildair continued to count.

"Eighty-nine, ninety, ninety-one - "

The tension became unbearable. Two or three voices protested against the needless prolonging of the torture.

"Ninety-six, ninety-seven, ninety-eight, ninety-nine and one hundred."

A match sputtered in Mrs. Kildair's hand and on the instant the company craned forward. In the center of the table was the sparkling sapphire and diamond ring. Candles were lit, flaring up like searchlights on the white accusing faces.

"Mr. Cheever, you may give it to me," said Mrs. Kildair. She held out her hand without trembling, a smile of triumph on her face, which had in it for a moment an expression of positive cruelty.

Immediately she changed, contemplating with amusement the horror of her guests, staring blindly from one to another, seeing the indefinable glance of interrogation that passed from Cheever to Mrs. Cheever, from Mrs. Jackson to her husband, and then without emotion she said:

"Now that that is over we can have a very gay little supper."

When Peters had pushed back his chair, satisfied as only a trained raconteur can be by the silence of a difficult audience, and had busied himself with a cigar, there was an instant outcry.

"I say, Peters, old boy, that is not all!"

"Absolutely."

"The story ends there?"

"That ends the story."

"But who took the ring?"

Peters extended his hands in an empty gesture.

"What! It was never found out?"

"Never."

"No clue?"

"None."

"I don't like the story," said De Gollyer.

"It's no story at all," said Steingall.

"Permit me," said Quinny in a didactic way; "it is a story, and it is complete. In fact, I consider it unique because it has none of the banalities of a solution and leaves the problem even more confused than at the start."

"I don't see - " began Rankin.

"Of course you don't, my dear man," said Quinny crushingly. "You do not see that any solution would be commonplace, whereas no solution leaves an extraordinary intellectual problem."

"How so?"

"In the first place," said Quinny, preparing to annex the topic, "whether the situation actually happened or not, which is in itself a mere triviality, Peters has constructed it in a masterly way, the proof of which is that he has made me listen. Observe, each person present might have taken the ring - Flanders, a broker, just come a cropper; Maude Lille, a woman on the ragged side of life in desperate means; either Mr. and Mrs. Cheever, suspected of being card sharps - very good touch that, Peters, when the husband and wife glanced involuntarily at each other at the end - Mr. Enos Jackson, a sharp lawyer, or his wife about to be divorced; even Harris, concerning whom, very cleverly, Peters has said nothing at all to make him quite the most suspicious of all. There are, therefore, seven solutions, all possible and all logical. But beyond this is left a great intellectual problem."

"How so?"

"Was it a feminine or a masculine action to restore the ring when threatened with a search, knowing that Mrs. Kildair's clever expedient of throwing the room in the dark made detection impossible? Was it a woman who lacked the necessary courage to continue, or was it a man who repented his first impulse? Is a man or is a woman the greater natural criminal?"

"A woman took it, of course," said Rankin.

"On the contrary, it was a man," said Steingall, "for the second action was more difficult than the first."

"A man, certainly," said De Gollyer. "The restoration of the ring was a logical decision."

"You see," said Quinny triumphantly, "personally I incline to a woman for the reason that a weaker feminine nature is peculiarly susceptible to the domination of her own sex. There you are. We could meet and debate the subject year in and year out and never agree."

"I recognize most of the characters," said De Gollyer with a little confidential smile toward Peters. "Mrs. Kildair, of course, is all you say of her - an extraordinary woman. The story is quite characteristic of her. Flanders, I am not sure of, but I think I know him."

"Did it really happen?" asked Rankin, who always took the commonplace point of view.

"Exactly as I have told it," said Peters.

"The only one I don't recognize is Harris," said De Gollyer pensively.

"Your humble servant," said Peters, smiling.

The four looked up suddenly with a little start.

"What!" said Quinny, abruptly confused. "You - you were there?"

"I was there."

The four continued to look at him without speaking, each absorbed in his own thoughts, with a sudden ill ease.

A club attendant with a telephone slip on a tray stopped by Peters' side. He excused himself and went along the porch, nodding from table to table.

"Curious chap," said De Gollyer musingly.

"Extraordinary."

The word was like a murmur in the group of four, who continued watching Peters' trim disappearing figure in silence, without looking at one another - with a certain ill ease.

A COMEDY FOR WIVES

At half-past six o'clock from Wall Street, Jack Lightbody let himself into his apartment, called his wife by name, and received no answer.

"Hello, that's funny," he thought, and, ringing, asked of the maid, "Did Mrs. Lightbody go out?"

"About an hour ago, sir."

"That's odd. Did she leave any message?"

"No, sir."

"That's not like her. I wonder what's happened."

At this moment his eye fell on an open hat-box of mammoth proportions, overshadowing a thin table in the living-room.

"When did that come?"

"About four o'clock, sir."

He went in, peeping into the empty box with a smile of satisfaction and understanding.

"That's it, she's rushed off to show it to some one," he

Owen Johnson

said, with a half vindictive look toward the box. "Well, it cost $175, and I don't get my winter suit; but I get a little peace."

He went to his room, rebelliously preparing to dress for the dinner and theater to which he had been commanded.

"By George, if I came back late, wouldn't I catch it?" he said with some irritation, slipping into his evening clothes and looking critically at his rather subdued reflection in the glass. "Jim tells me I'm getting in a rut, middle-aged, showing the wear. Perhaps." He rubbed his hand over the wrinkled cheek and frowned. "I have gone off a bit - sedentary life - six years. It does settle you. Hello! quarter of seven. Very strange!"

He slipped into a lilac dressing-gown which had been thrust upon him on his last birthday and wandered uneasily back into the dining-room.

"Why doesn't she telephone?" he thought; "it's her own party, one of those infernal problem plays I abhor. I didn't want to go."

The door opened and the maid entered. On the tray was a letter.

"For me?" he said, surprised. "By messenger?"

"Yes, sir."

He signed the slip, glancing at the envelope. It was in his wife's handwriting.

"Margaret!" he said suddenly.

"Yes, sir."

"The boy's waiting for an answer, isn't he?"

"No, sir."

He stood a moment in blank uneasiness, until, suddenly aware that she was waiting, he dismissed her with a curt:

"Oh, very well."

Then he remained by the table, looking at the envelope which he did not open, hearing the sound of the closing outer door and the passing of the maid down the hall.

"Why didn't she telephone?" he said aloud slowly.

He looked at the letter again. He had made no mistake. It was from his wife.

"If she's gone off again on some whim," he said angrily, "by George, I won't stand for it."

Then carelessly inserting a finger, he broke the cover and glanced hastily down the letter:

My dear Jackie:

When you have read this I shall have left you forever. Forget me and try to forgive. In the six years we have lived together, you have always been kind to me. But, Jack, there is something we cannot give or take away, and because some one has come who has won that, I am leaving you. I'm sorry, Jackie, I'm sorry.

Irene.

When he had read this once in unbelief, he read it immediately again, approaching the lamp, laying it on the table and pressing his fists against his temple, to concentrate all his mind.

"It's a joke," he said, speaking aloud.

He rose, stumbling a little and aiding himself with his arm, leaning against the wall, went into her room, and opened the drawer where her jewel case should be. It was gone.

"Then it's true," he said solemnly. "It's ended. What am I to do?"

He went to her wardrobe, looking at the vacant hooks, repeating:

"What am I to do?"

He went slowly back to the living-room to the desk by the lamp, where the hateful thing stared up at him.

"What am I to do?"

All at once he struck the desk with his fist and a cry burst from him:

"Dishonored - I'm dishonored!"

His head flushed hot, his breath came in short, panting rage. He struck the letter again and again, and then suddenly, frantically, began to rush back and forth, repeating:

"Dishonored - dishonored!"

All at once a moment of clarity came to him with a chill of ice. He stopped, went to the telephone and called up the Racquet Club, saying:

"Mr. De Gollyer to the 'phone."

Then he looked at his hand and found he was still clutching a forgotten hair brush. With a cry at the grotesqueness of the thing, he flung it from him, watching it go skipping over the polished floor. The voice of De Gollyer called him.

"Is that you, Jim?" he said, steadying himself. "Come - come to me at once - quick!"

He could have said no more. He dropped the receiver, overturning the stand, and began again his caged pacing of the floor.

Ten minutes later De Gollyer nervously slipped into the room. He was a quick, instinctive ferret of a man, one to whose eyes the hidden life of the city held no mysteries; who understood equally the shadows that glide on the street and the masks that pass in luxurious carriages. In one glance he had caught the disorder in the room and the agitation in his friend. He advanced a step, balanced his hat on the desk, perceived the crumpled letter, and, clearing his throat, drew back, frowning and alert, correctly prepared for any situation.

Lightbody, without seeming to perceive his arrival, continued his blind traveling, pressing his fists from time to time against his throat to choke back the excess of emotions which, in the last minutes, had dazed his perceptions and left him inertly struggling against a shapeless pain. All at once he stopped, flung out his arms and cried:

"She's gone!"

De Gollyer did not on the word seize the situation.

"Gone! Who's gone?" he said with a nervous, jerky fixing of his head, while his glance immediately sought the vista through the door to assure himself that no third person was present.

But Lightbody, unconscious of everything but his own utter grief, was threshing back and forth, repeating mechanically, with increasing *staccato*:

"Gone, gone!"

"Who? Where?"

With a sudden movement, De Gollyer caught his friend by the shoulder and faced him about as a naughty child, exclaiming: "Here, I say, old chap, brace up! Throw back your shoulders - take a long breath!"

With a violent wrench, Lightbody twisted himself free, while one hand flung appealingly back, begged for time to master the emotion which burst forth in the cry:

"Gone - forever!"

"By Jove!" said De Gollyer, suddenly enlightened, and through his mind flashed the thought - "There's been an accident - something fatal. Tough - devilish tough."

He cast a furtive glance toward the bedrooms and then an alarmed one toward his friend, standing in the embrasure of the windows, pressing his forehead against the panes.

Suddenly Lightbody turned and, going abruptly to the desk, leaned heavily on one arm, raising the letter in two vain efforts. A spasm of pain crossed his lips, which alone could not be controlled. He turned his head hastily, half offering, half dropping the letter, and wheeling, went to an armchair, where he collapsed, repeating inarticulately:

"Forever!"

"Who? What? Who's gone?" exclaimed De Gollyer, bewildered by the appearance of a letter. "Good heavens, dear boy, what has happened? Who's gone?"

Then Lightbody, by an immense effort, answered:

"Irene - my wife!"

And with a rapid motion he covered his eyes, digging his fingers into his flesh.

De Gollyer, pouncing upon the letter, read:

My dear Jackie: When you read this, I shall have left you forever -

Then he halted with an exclamation, and hastily turned

the page for the signature.

"Read!" said Lightbody in a stifled voice.

"I say, this is serious, devilishly serious," said De Gollyer, now thoroughly amazed. Immediately he began to read, unconsciously emphasizing the emphatic words - a little trick of his enunciation.

When Lightbody had heard from the voice of another the message that stood written before his eyes, all at once all impulses in his brain converged into one. He sprang up, speaking now in quick, distinct syllables, sweeping the room with the fury of his arms.

"I'll find them; by God, I'll find them. I'll hunt them down. I'll follow them. I'll track them - anywhere - to the ends of the earth - and when I find them - "

De Gollyer, sensitively distressed at such a scene, vainly tried to stop him.

"I'll find them, if I die for it! I'll shoot them down. I'll shoot them down like dogs! I will, by all that's holy, I will! I'll butcher them! I'll shoot them down, there at my feet, rolling at my feet!"

All at once he felt a weight on his arm, and heard De Gollyer saying, vainly:

"Dear boy, be calm, be calm."

"Calm!" he cried, with a scream, his anger suddenly focusing on his friend, "Calm! I won't be calm! What! I come back - slaving all day, slaving for her - come back to take her out to dinner where she wants to go - to the play she wants to see, and I find - nothing - this letter - this bomb - this thunderbolt! Everything gone - my home broken up - my name dishonored - my whole life ruined! And you say be calm - be calm - be calm!"

Then, fearing the hysteria gaining possession of him, he dropped back violently into an armchair and covered his face.

During this outburst, De Gollyer had deliberately removed his gloves, folded them and placed them in his breast pocket. His reputation for social omniscience had been attained by the simple expedient of never being convinced. As soon as the true situation had been unfolded, a slight, skeptical smile hovered about his thin, flouting lips, and, looking at his old friend, he was not unpleasantly aware of something comic in the attitudes of grief. He made one or two false starts, buttoning his trim cutaway, and then said in a purposely higher key:

"My dear old chap, we must consider - we really must consider what is to be done."

"There is only one thing to be done," cried Lightbody in a voice of thunder.

"Permit me!"

"Kill them!"

"One moment!"

De Gollyer, master of himself, never abandoning his critical enjoyment, softened his voice to that controlled note that is the more effective for being opposed to frenzy.

"Sit down - come now, sit down!"

Lightbody resisted.

"Sit down, there - come - you have called me in. Do you want my advice? Do you? Well, just quiet down. Will you listen?"

"I am quiet," said Lightbody, suddenly submissive. The frenzy of his rage passed, but to make his resolution doubly impressive, he extended his arm and said slowly:

"But remember, my mind is made up. I shall not budge. I shall shoot them down like dogs! You see I say quietly - like dogs!"

"My dear old pal," said De Gollyer with a well-bred shrug of his shoulders, "you'll do nothing of the sort. We are men of the world, my boy, men of the world. Shooting is archaic - for the rural districts. We've progressed way beyond that - men of the world don't shoot any more."

"I said it quietly," said Lightbody, who perceived, not without surprise, that he was no longer at the same temperature. However, he concluded with normal conviction: "I shall kill them both, that's all. I say it quietly."

This gave De Gollyer a certain hortatory moment of which he availed himself, seeking to reduce further the dramatic tension.

"My dear old pal, as a matter of fact, all I say is, consider first and shoot after. In the first place, suppose you kill one or both and you are not yourself killed - for you know, dear boy, the deuce is that sometimes does happen. What then? Justice is so languid nowadays. Certainly you would have to inhabit for six, eight - perhaps ten months - a drafty, moist jail, without exercise, most indigestible food abominably cooked, limited society. You are brought to trial. A jury - an emotional jury - may give you a couple of years. That's another risk. You see you drink cocktails, you smoke cigarettes. You will be made to appear a person totally unfit to live with."

Lightbody with a movement of irritation, shifted the clutch of his fingers.

"As a matter of fact, suppose you are acquitted, what then? You emerge, middle-aged, dyspeptic, possibly rheumatic - no nerves left. Your photograph figures in every paper along with inventors of shoes and corsets. You can't be asked to dinner or to house parties, can you? As a matter of fact, you'll disappear somewhere or linger and get shot by the brother, who in turn, as soon as he is acquitted, must be shot by your brother, et cetera, et cetera! *Voila!* What will you have gained?"

He ceased, well pleased - he had convinced himself.

Lightbody, who had had time to be ashamed of the emotion that he, as a man, had shown to another of his sex, rose and said with dignity:

"I shall have avenged my honor."

De Gollyer, understanding at once that the battle had

Owen Johnson

been won, took up in an easy running attack his battery of words.

"By publishing your dishonor to Europe, Africa, Asia? That's logic, isn't it? No, no, my dear old Jack - you won't do it. You won't be an ass. Steady head, old boy! Let's look at it in a reasonable way - as men of the world. You can't bring her back, can you? She's gone."

At this reminder, overcome by the vibrating sense of loss, Lightbody turned abruptly, no longer master of himself, and going hastily toward the windows, cried violently:

"Gone!"

Over the satisfied lips of De Gollyer the same ironical smile returned.

"I say, as a matter of fact I didn't suspect, you - you cared so much."

"I adored her!"

With a quick movement, Lightbody turned. His eyes flashed. He no longer cared what he revealed. He began to speak incoherently, stifling a sob at every moment.

"I adored her. It was wonderful. Nothing like it. I adored her from the moment I met her. It was that - adoration - one woman in the world - one woman - I adored her!"

The imp of irony continued to play about De Gollyer's eyes and slightly twitching lips.

"Quite so - quite so," he said. "Of course you know, dear boy, you weren't always so - so lonely - the old days - you surprise me."

The memory of his romance all at once washed away the bitterness in Lightbody. He returned, sat down, oppressed, crushed.

"You know, Jim," he said solemnly, "she never did this, never in the world, not of her own free will, never in her right mind. She's been hypnotized, some one has gotten her under his power - some scoundrel. No - I'll not harm her, I'll not hurt a hair of her head - but when I meet *him* - "

"By the way, whom do you suspect?" said De Gollyer, who had long withheld the question.

"Whom? Whom do I suspect?" exclaimed Lightbody, astounded. "I don't know."

"Impossible!"

"How do I know? I never doubted her a minute."

"Yes, yes - still?"

"Whom do I suspect? I don't know." He stopped and considered. "It might be - three men."

"Three men!" exclaimed De Gollyer, who smiled as only a bachelor could smile at such a moment.

"I don't know which - how should I know? But when I do know - when I meet him! I'll spare her - but - but when we meet - we two - when my hands are on

Owen Johnson

his throat - "

He was on his feet again, the rage of dishonor ready to flame forth. De Gollyer, putting his arm about him, recalled him with abrupt, military sternness.

"Steady, steady again, dear old boy. Buck up now - get hold of yourself."

"Jim, it's awful!"

"It's tough - very tough!"

"Out of a clear sky - everything gone!"

"Come, now, walk up and down a bit - do you good."

Lightbody obeyed, locking his arms behind his back, his eyes on the floor.

"Everything smashed to bits!"

"You adored her?" questioned De Gollyer in an indefinable tone.

"I adored her!" replied Lightbody explosively.

"Really now?"

"I adored her. There's nothing left now - nothing - nothing."

"Steady."

Lightbody, at the window, made another effort, controlled himself and said, as a man might renounce an inheritance:

"You're right, Jim - but it's hard."

"Good spirit - fine, fine, very fine!" commented De Gollyer in critical enthusiasm, "nothing public, eh? No scandal - not our class. Men of the world. No shooting! People don't shoot any more. It's reform, you know, for the preservation of bachelors."

The effort, the renunciation of his just vengeance, had exhausted Lightbody, who turned and came back, putting out his hands to steady himself.

"It isn't that, it's, it's - " Suddenly his fingers encountered on the table a pair of gloves - his wife's gloves, forgotten there. He raised them, holding them in his open palm, glanced at De Gollyer and, letting them fall, suddenly unable to continue, turned aside his head.

"Take time - a good breath," said De Gollyer, in military fashion, "fill your lungs. Splendid! That's it."

Lightbody, sitting down at the desk, wearily drew the gloves to him, gazing fixedly at the crushed perfumed fingers.

"Why, Jim," he said finally, "I adore her so - if she can be happier - happier with another - if that will make her happier than I can make her - well, I'll step aside, I'll make no trouble - just for her, just for what she's done for me."

The last words were hardly heard. This time, despite himself, De Gollyer was tremendously affected.

"Superb! By George, that's grit!"

Lightbody raised his head with the fatigue of the struggle and the pride of the victory written on it.

"Her happiness first," he said simply.

The accent with which it was spoken almost convinced De Gollyer.

"By Jove, you adore her!"

"I adore her," said Lightbody, lifting himself to his feet. This time it came not as an explosion, but as a breath, some deep echo from the soul. He stood steadily gazing at his friend. "You're right, Jim. You're right. It's not our class. I'll face it down. There'll be no scandal. No one shall know."

Their hands met with an instinctive motion. Then, touched by the fervor of his friend's admiration, Lightbody moved wearily away, saying dully, all in a breath:

"Like a thunderclap, Jim."

"I know, dear old boy," said De Gollyer, feeling sharply vulnerable in the eyes and throat.

"It's terrible - it's awful. All in a second! Everything turned upside down, everything smashed!"

"You must go away," said De Gollyer anxiously.

"My whole life wrecked," continued Lightbody, without hearing him, " nothing left - not the slightest, meanest thing left!"

"Dear boy, you must go away."

"Only last night she was sitting here, and I there, reading a book." He stopped and put forth his hand. "This book!"

"Jack, you must go away for a while."

"What?"

"Go away!"

"Oh, yes, yes. I suppose so. I don't care."

Leaning against the desk, he gazed down at the rug, mentally and physically inert.

De Gollyer, returning to his nature, said presently: "I say, dear old fellow, it's awfully delicate, but I should like to be frank, from the shoulder - out and out, do you mind?"

"What? No."

Seeing that Lightbody had only half listened, De Gollyer spoke with some hesitation:

"Of course it's devilish impudent. I'll offend you dreadfully. But, I say, now as a matter of fact, were you really so - so seraphically happy?"

"What's that?"

"As a matter of fact," said De Gollyer changing his

note instantly, "you were happy, *terrifically* happy, *always* happy, weren't you?"

Lightbody was indignant.

"Oh, how can you, at such a moment?"

The new emotion gave him back his physical elasticity. He began to pace up and down, declaiming at his friend, "I was happy, *ideally* happy. I never had a thought, not one, for anything else. I gave her everything. I did everything she wanted. There never was a word between us. It was *ideal*"

De Gollyer, somewhat shamefaced, avoiding his angry glance, said hastily:

"So, so, I was quite wrong. I beg your pardon."

"*Ideally* happy," continued Lightbody, more insistently. "We had the same thoughts, the same tastes, we read the same books. She had a mind, a wonderful mind. It was an *ideal* union."

"The devil, I may be all wrong," thought De Gollyer to himself. He crossed his arms, nodded his head, and this time it was with the profoundest conviction that he repeated:

"You adored her."

"I *adored* her," said Lightbody, with a ring to his voice. "Not a word against her, not a word. It was not her fault. I know it's not her fault."

" You must go away," said De Gollyer, touching him

on the shoulder.

"Oh, I must! I couldn't stand it here in this room," said Lightbody bitterly. His fingers wandered lightly over the familiar objects on the desk, shrinking from each fiery contact. He sat down. "You're right, I must get away."

"You're dreadfully hard hit, aren't you?"

"Oh, Jim!"

Lightbody's hand closed over the book and he opened it mechanically in the effort to master the memory. "This book - we were reading it last night together."

"Jack, look here," said De Gollyer, suddenly unselfish before such a great grief, "you've got to be bucked up, boy, pulled together. I'll tell you what I'll do. You're going to get right off. You're going to be looked after. I'll knock off myself. I'll take you."

Lightbody gave him his hand with a dumb, grateful look that brought a quick lump to the throat of De Gollyer, who, in terror, purposely increasing the lightness of his manner, sprang up with exaggerated gaiety.

"By Jove, fact is, I'm a bit dusty myself. Do me good. We'll run off just as we did in the old days - good days, those. We knocked about a bit, didn't we? Good days, eh, Jack?"

Lightbody, continuing to gaze at the book, said:

"Last night - only last night! Is it possible?"

"Come, now, let's polish off Paris, or Vienna?"

"No, no." Lightbody seemed to shrink at the thought. "Not that, nothing gay. I couldn't bear to see others gay - happy."

"Quite right. California?"

"No, no, I want to get away, out of the country - far away."

Suddenly an inspiration came to De Gollyer - a memory of earlier days.

"By George, Morocco! Superb! The trip we planned out - Morocco - the very thing!"

Lightbody, at the desk still feebly fingering the leaves that he indistinctly saw, muttered:

"Something far away - away from people."

"By George, that's immense," continued De Gollyer exploding with delight, and, on a higher octave, he repeated: "Immense! Morocco and a smashing dash into Africa for big game. The old trip just as we planned it seven years ago. IMMENSE!"

"I don't care - anywhere."

De Gollyer went nimbly to the bookcase and bore back an atlas.

"My boy - the best thing in the world. Set you right up - terrific air, smashing scenery, ripping sport, caravans and all that sort of thing. Fine idea, very fine.

Never could forgive you breaking up that trip, you know. There." Rapidly he skimmed through the atlas, mumbling, "M-M-M - Morocco."

Lightbody, irritated at the idea of facing a decision, moved uneasily, saying, "Anywhere, anywhere."

"Back into harness again - the old camping days - immense."

"I must get away."

"There you are," said De Gollyer at length. With a deft movement he slipped the atlas in front of his friend, saying, "Morocco, devilish smart air, smashing colors, blues and reds."

"Yes, yes."

"You remember how we planned it," continued De Gollyer, artfully blundering; "boat to Tangier, from Tangier bang across to Fez."

At this Lightbody, watching the tracing finger, said with some irritation, "No, no, down the coast first."

"I beg your pardon," said De Gollyer; "to Fez, my dear fellow."

"My dear boy, I know! Down the coast to Rabat."

"Ah, now, you're sure? I think - "

"And I *know*," said Lightbody, raising his voice and assuming possession of the atlas, which he struck energetically with the back of his hand. "I ought to know my own plan."

"Yes, yes," said De Gollyer, to egg him on. "Still you're thoroughly convinced about that, are you?"

"Of course, I am! My dear Jim - come, isn't this my pet idea - the one trip I've dreamed over, the one thing in the world I've longed to do, all my life?" His eyes took energy, while his forefinger began viciously to stab the atlas. "We go to Rabat. We go to Magazam, and we cut - so - long sweep, into the interior, take a turn, so, and back to Fez, so!"

This speech, delivered with enthusiasm, made De Gollyer reflect. He looked at the somewhat revived Lightbody with thoughtful curiosity.

"Well, well - you may be right. You always are impressive, you know."

"Right? Of course I'm right," continued Lightbody, unaware of his friend's critical contemplation. "Haven't I worked out every foot of it?"

"A bit of a flyer in the game country, then? Topple over a rhino or so. Stunning, smart sport, the rhino!"

"By George, think of it - a chance at one of the brutes!"

When De Gollyer had seen the eagerness in his friend's eyes, the imps returned, ironically tumbling back. He slapped him on the shoulder as Mephistopheles might gleefully claim his own, crying, "Immense!"

"You know, Jim," said Lightbody, straightening up, nervously alert, speaking in quick, eager accents, "it's what I've dreamed of - a chance at one of the big beggars. By George, I have, all my life!"

"We'll polish it off in ripping style, regiments of porters, red and white tents, camels, caravans and all that sort of thing."

"By George, just think of it."

"In style, my boy - we'll own the whole continent, buy it up!"

"The devil!"

"What's the matter?"

Lightbody's mood had suddenly dropped. He half pushed back his chair and frowned. "It's going to be frightfully extravagant."

"What of it?"

"My dear fellow, you don't know what my expenses are - this apartment, an automobile - Oh, as for you, it's all very well for you! You have ten thousand a year and no one to care for but yourself."

Suddenly he felt almost a hatred for his friend, and then a rebellion at the renunciation he would have to make.

"No - it can't be done. We'll have to give it up. Impossible, utterly impossible, I can't afford it."

De Gollyer, still a little uncertain of his ground, for several moments waited, carefully considering the dubious expression on his friend's face. Then he questioned abruptly:

"What is your income - now?"

"What do you mean by *now*?"

"Fifteen thousand a year?"

"It has always been that," replied Lightbody in bad humor.

De Gollyer, approaching at last the great question, assumed an air of concentrated firmness, tempered with well-mannered delicacy.

"My dear boy, I beg your pardon. As a matter of fact it has always been fifteen thousand - quite right, quite so; but - now, my dear boy, you are too much of a man of the world to be offended, aren't you?"

"No," said Lightbody, staring in front of him. "No, I'm not offended."

"Of course it's delicate, ticklishly delicate ground, but then we must look things in the face. Now if you'd rather I - "

"No, go on."

"Of course, dear boy, you've had a smashing knock and all that sort of thing, but - " suddenly reaching out he took up the letter, and, letting it hang from his fingers, thoughtfully considered it - "I say it might be looked at in this way. Yesterday it was fifteen thousand a year to dress up a dashing wife, modern

New York style, the social pace, clothes that must be smarter than Thingabob's wife, competitive dinners that you stir up with your fork and your servants eat, and all that sort of thing, you know. To-day it's fifteen thousand a year and a bachelor again."

Releasing the letter, he disdainfully allowed it to settle down on the desk, and finished:

"Come now, as a matter of fact there is a little something consoling, isn't there?"

From the moment he had perceived De Gollyer's idea. Lightbody had become very quiet, gazing steadily ahead, seeing neither the door nor the retaining walls.

"I never thought of that," he said, almost in a whisper.

"Quite so, quite so. Of course one doesn't think of such things, right at first. And you've had a knock-down - a regular smasher, old chap." He stopped, cleared his voice and said sympathetically: "You adored her?"

"I suppose I could give up the apartment and sell the auto," said Lightbody slowly, speaking to himself.

De Gollyer smiled - a bachelor smile.

"Riches, my boy," he said, tapping him on the shoulder with the same quick, awakening Mephistophelean touch.

The contact raised Lightbody from revery. He drew back, shocked at the ways through which his thoughts had wandered.

Owen Johnson

"No, no, Jim," he said. "No, you mustn't, nothing like that - not at such a time."

"You're right," said De Gollyer, instantly masked in gravity. "You're quite right. Still, we are looking things in the face - planning for the future. Of course it's a delicate question, terrifically delicate. I'm almost afraid to put it to you. Come, now, how shall I express it - delicately? It's this way. Fifteen thousand a year divided by one is fifteen thousand, isn't it; but fifteen thousand a year divided by two, may mean -" He straightened up, heels clicking, throwing out his elbows slightly and lifting his chin from the high, white stockade on which it reposed. "Come, now, we're men of the world, aren't we? Now, as a matter of fact how much of that fifteen thousand a year came back to you?"

"My dear Jim," said Lightbody, feeling that generosity should be his part, "a woman, a modern woman, a New York woman, you just said it - takes - takes - "

"Twelve thousand - thirteen thousand?"

"Oh, come! Nonsense," said Lightbody, growing quite angry. "Besides, I don't - "

"Yes, yes, I know," said De Gollyer, interrupting him, now with fresh confidence. "All the same your whiskies have gone off, dear boy - they've gone off, and your cigars are bad, very bad. Little things, but they show."

A pencil lay before him. Lightbody, without knowing what he did, took it up and mechanically on an unwritten sheet jotted down $15,000, drawing the dollar sign with a careful, almost caressing stroke. The sheet was the back of his wife's letter, but he did not notice it.

De Gollyer, looking over his shoulder, exclaimed:

"Quite right. Fifteen thousand, divided by one."

"It will make a difference," said Lightbody slowly. Over his face passed an expression such as comes but once in a lifetime; a look defying analysis; a look that sweeps back over the past and challenges the future and always retains the secret of its judgment.

De Gollyer, drawing back slowly, allowed him a moment before saying:

"And no alimony!"

"What?"

"Free and no alimony, my boy!"

"No alimony?" said Lightbody, surprised at this new reasoning.

"A woman who runs away gets no alimony," said De Gollyer loudly. "Not here, not in the effete East!"

"I hadn't thought of that, either," said Lightbody, who, despite himself, could not repress a smile.

De Gollyer, irritated perhaps that he should have been duped into sympathy, ran on with a little vindictiveness.

"Of course that means nothing to you, dear boy. You were happy, *ideally* happy! You adored her, didn't you?"

He paused and then, receiving no reply, continued:

"But you see, if you hadn't been so devilish lucky, so seraphically happy all these years, you might find a certain humor in the situation, mightn't you? Still, look it in the face, what have you lost, what have you left? There is something in that. Fifteen thousand a year, liberty and no alimony."

The moment had come which could no longer be evaded. Lightbody rose, turned, met the lurking malice in De Gollyer's eyes with the blank indecision screen of his own, and, turning on his heel, went to a little closet in the wall, and bore back a decanter and glasses.

"This is not what we serve on the table," he said irrelevantly. "It's whisky."

De Gollyer poured out his drink and looked at Lightbody *en connoisseur*.

"You've gone off - old - six years. You were the smartest of the old crowd, too. You certainly have gone off."

Lightbody listened, with his eyes in his glass.

"Jack, you're middle-aged - you've gone off - badly. It's hit you hard."

There was a moment's silence and then Lightbody

spoke quietly:

"Jim!"

"What is it, old boy?"

"Do you want to know the truth?"

"Come - out with it!"

Lightbody struggled a moment, all the hesitation showing in his lips. Then he said, slowly shaking his head, never lifting his eyes, speaking as though to another:

"Jim, I've had a hell of a time!"

"Impossible!"

"Yes."

He lifted his glass until he felt its touch against his lips and gradually set it down. "Why, Jim, in six years I've loved her so that I've never done anything I wanted to do, gone anywhere I wanted to go, drank anything I've wanted to drink, saw anything I wanted to see, wore anything I wanted to wear, smoked anything I wanted to smoke, read anything I wanted to read, or dined any one I wanted to dine! Jim, it certainly has been a *domestic* time!"

"Good God! I can't believe it!" ejaculated De Gollyer, too astounded to indulge his sense of humor.

All at once a little fury seemed to seize Lightbody. His voice rose and his gestures became indignant.

"Married! I've been married to a policeman. Why, Jim, do you know what I've spent on myself, really spent? Not two thousand, not one thousand, not five hundred dollars a year. I've been poorer than my own clerk. I'd hate to tell you what I paid for cigars and whisky. Everything went to her, everything! And Jim -" he turned suddenly with a significant glance - "such a temper!"

"A temper? No, impossible, not that!"

"Not violent - oh, no - but firm - smiling, you know, but irresistible."

He drew a long breath charged with bitter memories and said between his teeth, rebelling: "I always agreed."

"Can it be? Is it possible?" commented De Gollyer, carefully mastering his expression.

Lightbody, on the new subject of his wrongs, now began to explode with wrath.

"And there's one thing more - one thing that hurts! You know what she eloped in? She eloped in a hat, a big red hat, three white feathers - one hundred and seventy-five dollars. I gave up a winter suit to get it."

He strode over to the grotesquely large hat-box on the slender table, and struck it with his fist.

"Came this morning. Jim, she waited for that hat! Now, that isn't right! That isn't delicate!"

"No, by Jove, it certainly isn't delicate!"

"Domesticity! Ha!" At the moment, with only the long vision of petty tyranny before him, he could have caught her up in his hands and strangled her. "Domesticity! I've had all I want of domesticity!"

Suddenly the eternal fear awakening in him, he turned and commanded authoritatively:

"Never tell!"

"Never!"

De Gollyer, at forty-two, showed a responsive face, invincibly, gravely sympathetic, patiently awaiting his climax, knowing that nothing is so cumulatively dangerous as confession.

Lightbody took up his glass and again approached it to his lips, frowning at the thought of what he had revealed. All at once a fresh impulse caught him, he put down his glass untasted, blurting out:

"Do you want to know one thing more? Do you want to know the truth, the real truth?"

"Gracious heavens, there is something more?"

"I never married her - never in God's world!"

He ceased and suddenly, not to be denied, the past ranged itself before him in its stark verity.

"She married me!"

"Is it possible?"

"She did!"

What had been an impulse suddenly became a certainty.

"As I look back now, I can see it all - quite clear. Do you know how it happened? I called three times - not one time more - three times! I liked her - nothing more. She was an attractive-looking girl - a certain fascination - she always has that - that's the worst of it - but gentle, very gentle."

"Extraordinary!"

"On the third time I called - the third time, mind you," proceeded Lightbody, attacking the table, "as I stood up to say good-by, all at once - the lights went out."

"The lights?"

"When they went on again - I was engaged."

"Great heavens!"

"The old fainting trick."

"Is it possible?"

"I see it all now. A man sees things as they are at such a moment."

He gave a short, disagreeable laugh. "Jim, she had those lights all fixed!"

"Frightful!"

Lightbody, who had stripped his soul in confession, no longer was conscious of shame. He struck the table, punctuating his wrath, and cried:

"And that's the truth! The solemn literal truth! That's my story!"

To confess, it had been necessary to be swept away in a burst of anger. The necessity having ceased, he crossed his arms, quite calm, laughing a low, scornful laugh.

"My dear boy," said De Gollyer, to relieve the tension, "as a matter of fact, that's the way you're all caught."

"I believe it," said Lightbody curtly. He had now an instinctive desire to insult the whole female sex.

"I know - a bachelor knows. The things I have seen and the things I have heard. My dear fellow, as a matter of fact, marriage is all very well for bankers and brokers, unconvicted millionaires, week domestic animals in search of a capable housekeeper, you know, and all that sort of thing, but for men of the world – like ourselves, it's a mistake. Don't do it again, my boy - don't do it."

Lightbody laughed a barking laugh that quite satisfied De Gollyer.

"Husbands - modern social husbands - are excrescences - they don't count. They're mere financial tabulators - nothing more than social sounding-boards."

"Right!" said Lightbody savagely.

"Ah, you like that, do you?" said De Gollyer, pleased. "I do say a good thing occasionally. Social sounding-boards! Why, Jack, in one-half of the marriages in this country - no, by George, in two-thirds - if the inconsequential, tabulating husband should come home to find a letter like this - he'd be dancing a *can-can*!"

Lightbody felt a flood of soul-easing laughter well up within him. He bit his lip and answered:

"No!"

"Yes."

"Pshaw!"

"A *can-can*!"

Lightbody, fearing to betray himself, did not dare to look at the triumphant bachelor. He covered his eyes with his hands and sought to fight down the joyful hysteria that began to shake his whole body. All at once he caught sight of De Gollyer's impish eyes, and, unable longer to contain himself, burst out laughing. The more he laughed at De Gollyer, who laughed back at him, the more uncontrollable he became. Tears came to his eyes and trickled down his cheeks, washing away all illusions and self-deception, leaving only the joy of deliverance, acknowledged at last.

All at once holding his sides, he found a little breath and cried combustibly:

"A *can-can*!"

Suddenly, with one impulse, they locked arms and

pirouetted about the room, flinging out destructive legs, hugging each other with bear-like hugs as they had done in college days of triumph. Exhausted at last, they reeled apart, and fell breathless into opposite chairs. There was a short moment of weak, physical silence, and then Lightbody, shaking his head, said solemnly:

"Jim - Jim, that's the first real genuine laugh I've had in six vast years!"

"My boy, it won't be the last."

"You bet it won't!" Lightbody sprang up, as out of the ashen cloak of age the young Faust springs forth. "To-morrow - do you hear, to-morrow we're off for Morocco!"

"By way of Paris?" questioned De Gollyer, who likewise gained a dozen years of youthfulness.

"Certainly by way of Paris."

"With a dash of Vienna?"

"Run it off the map!"

"Good old Jack! You're coming back, my boy, you're coming strong!"

"Am I? Just watch!" Dancing over to the desk, he seized a dozen heavy books:

"'Evolution and Psychology,' 'Burning Questions!' 'Woman's Position in Tasmania!' Aha!"

One by one, he flung them viciously over his head, reckoning not the crash with which they fell. Then with the same *pas de ballet* he descended on the hat-box and sent it from his boot crashing over the piano. Before De Gollyer could exclaim, he was at the closet, working havoc with the boxes of cigars.

"Here, I say," said De Gollyer laughing, "look out, those are cigars!"

"No, they're not," said Lightbody, pausing for a moment. Then, seizing two boxes, he whirled about the room holding them at arms' length, scattering them like the sparks of a pin-wheel, until with a final motion he flung the emptied boxes against the ceiling, and, coming to an abrupt stop, shot out a mandatory forefinger, and cried:

"Jim, you dine with me!"

"The fact is - "

"No buts, no excuses! Break all engagements! To-night we celebrate!"

"Immense!"

"Round up the boys - all the boys - the old crowd. I'm middle-aged, am I?"

"By George," said De Gollyer, in free admiration, "you're getting into form, my boy, excellent form. Fine, fine, very fine!"

"In half an hour at the Club."

"Done."

"Jim?"

"Jack!"

They precipitated themselves into each other's arms. Lightbody, as delirious as a young girl at the thought of her first ball, cried:

"Paris, Vienna, Morocco - two years around the world!"

"On my honor!"

Rapidly Lightbody, impatient for the celebration, put De Gollyer into his coat and armed him with his cane.

"In half an hour, Jim. Get Budd, get Reggie Long-worth, and, I say, get that little reprobate of a Smithy, will you?"

"Yes, by George."

At the door, De Gollyer, who, when he couldn't leave on an epigram, liked to recall the best thing he had said, turned:

"Never again, eh, old boy?"

"Never," cried Lightbody, with the voice of a cannon.

"No social sounding-board for us, eh?"

"Never again!"

"You do like that, don't you? I say a good thing now and then, don't I?"

Lightbody, all eagerness, drove him down the hall, crying:

"Round 'em up - round them all up! I'll show them if I've come back!"

When he had returned, waltzing on his toes to the middle of the room, he stopped and flung out his arms in a free gesture, inhaling a delicious breath. Then, whistling busily, he went to a drawer in the book-shelves and came lightly back, his arms crowded with time-tables, schedules of steamers, maps of various countries. All at once, remembering, he seized the telephone and, receiving no response, rang impatiently.

"Central - hello - hello! Central, why don't you answer? Central, give me - give me - hold up, wait a second!" He had forgotten the number of his own club. In communication at last, he heard the well-modulated accents of Rudolph - Rudolph who recognized his voice after six years. It gave him a little thrill, this reminder of the life he was entering once more. He ordered one of the dinners he used to order, and hung up the receiver, with a smile and a little tightening about his heart at the entry he, the prodigal, would make that night at the Club.

Then, seizing a map of Morocco in one hand and a schedule of sailings in the other, he sat down to plan, chanting over and over, "Paris, Vienna, Morocco, India, Paris, Vienna - "

At this moment, unnoticed by him, the doors moved

noiselessly and Mrs. Lightbody entered; a woman full of appealing movements in her lithe body, and of quick, decisive perceptions in the straight, gray glance of her eyes. She held with one hand a cloak fastened loosely about her throat. On her head was the hat with the three white feathers.

A minute passed while she stood, rapidly seizing every indication that might later assist her. Then she moved slightly and said in a voice of quiet sadness:

"Jackie."

"Great God!"

Lightbody, overturning chair and table, sprang up - recoiling as one recoils before an avenging specter. In his convulsive fingers were the time-tables, clinging like damp lily pads.

"Jackie, I couldn't do it. I couldn't abandon you. I've come back." Gently, seeming to move rather than to walk, advancing with none of the uncertainty that was in her voice, she cried, with a little break: "Forgive me!"

"No, no, never!"

He retreated behind a chair, fury in his voice, weak at the thought of the floating, entangling scarf, and the perfume he knew so well. Then, recovering himself, he cried brutally:

"Never! You have given me my freedom. I'll keep it! Thanks!"

With a gradual motion, she loosened her filmy cloak and let it slip from the suddenly revealed shoulders and slender body.

"No, no, I forbid you!" he cried. Anger - animal, instinctive anger - began to possess him. He became brutal as he felt himself growing weak.

"Either you go out or I do!"

"You will listen."

"What? To lies?"

"When you have heard me, you will understand, Jack."

"There is nothing to be said. I have not the slightest intention of taking back - "

"Jack!"

Her voice rang out with sudden impressiveness: "I swear to you I have not met him, I swear to you I came back of my own free will, because I could not meet him, because I found that it was you - you only - whom I wanted!"

"That is a lie!"

She recoiled before the wound in his glance. She put her long white hand over her heart, throwing all of herself into the glance that sought to conquer him.

"I swear it," she said simply.

"Another lie!"

"Jack!"

It was a physical rage that held him now, a rage divided against itself - that longed to strike down, to crush, to stifle the thing it coveted. He had almost a fear of himself. He cried:

"If you don't go, I'll - I'll - "

Suddenly he found something more brutal than a blow, something that must drive her away, while yet he had the strength of his passion. He crossed his arms, looking at her with a cold look.

"I'll tell you why you came back. You went to him for just one reason. You thought he had more money than I had. You came back when you found he hadn't."

He saw her body quiver and it did him good.

"That ends it," she said, hardly able to speak. She dropped her head hastily, but not before he had seen the tears.

"Absolutely."

In a moment she would be gone. He felt all at once uneasy, ashamed - she seemed so fragile.

"My cloak - give me my cloak," she said, and her voice showed that she accepted his verdict.

He brought the cloak to where she stood wearily, and put it on her shoulders, stepping back instantly.

"Good-by."

It was said more to the room than to him.

"Good-by," he said dully.

She took a step and then raised her eyes to his.

"That was more than you had a right to say, even to me," she said without reproach in her voice.

He avoided her look.

"You will be sorry. I know you," she said with pity for him. She went toward the door.

"I am sorry," he said impulsively. "I shouldn't have said it."

"Thank you," she said, stopping and returning a little toward him.

He drew back as though already he felt her arms about him.

"Don't," she said, smiling a tired smile. "I'm not going to try that."

Her instinct had given her possession of the scene. He felt it and was irritated.

"Only let us part quietly - with dignity," she said, "for we have been happy together for six years." Then she said rapidly:

"I want you to know that I shall do nothing to dishonor your name. I am not going to him. That is ended."

An immense curiosity came to him to learn the reason of this strange avowal. But he realized it would never do for him to ask it.

"Good-by, Jackie," she said, having waited a moment. "I shall not see you again."

He watched her leaving with the same moving grace with which she had come. All at once he found a way of evasion.

"Why don't you go to him?" he said harshly.

She stopped but did not turn.

"No," she said, shaking her head. And again she dared to continue toward the door.

"I shall not stand in your way," he said curtly, fearing only that she would leave. "I will give you a divorce. I don't deny a woman's liberty."

She turned, saying:

"Do you allow a woman liberty to know her own mind?"

"What do you mean?"

She came back until he almost could have touched her, standing looking into his eyes with a wistful, searching glance, clasping and unclasping her tense fingers.

"Jack," she said, "you never really cared."

" So it is all my fault!" he cried, snapping his arms

together, sure now that she would stay.

"Yes, it is."

"What!" he cried in a rage - already it was a different rage - "didn't I give you anything you wanted, everything I had, all my time, all - "

"All but yourself," she said quietly; "you were always cold."

"I!"

"You were! You were!" she said sharply, annoyed at the contradiction. But quickly remembering herself, she continued with only a regretful sadness in her voice:

"Always cold, always matter-of-fact. Bob of the head in the morning, jerk of the head at night. When I was happy over a new dress or a new hat you never noticed it - until the bill came in. You were always matter-of-fact, absolutely confident I was yours, body and soul."

"By George, that's too much!" he cried furiously. "That's a fine one. I'm to blame - of course I'm to blame!"

She drew a step away from him, and said:

"Listen! No, listen quietly, for when I've told you I shall go."

Despite himself, his anger vanished at her quiet command.

"If I listen," he thought, "it's all over."

He still believed he was resisting, only he wanted to hear as he had never wanted anything else - to learn why she was not going to the other man.

"Yes, what has happened is only natural," she said, drawing her eyebrows a little together and seeming to reason more with herself. "It had to happen before I could really be sure of my love for you. You men know and choose from the knowledge of many women. A woman, such as I, coming to you as a girl, must often and often ask herself if she would still make the same choice. Then another man comes into her life and she makes of him a test to know once and for all the answer to her question. Jack, that was it. That was the instinct that drove me to try if I *could* leave you - the instinct I did not understand then, but that I do now, when it's too late."

"Yes, she is clever," he thought to himself, listening to her, desiring her the more as he admired what he did not credit. He felt that he wanted to be convinced and with a last angry resistance, said:

"Very clever, indeed!"

She looked at him with her clear, gray look, a smile in her eyes, sadness on her lips.

"You know it is true."

He did not reply. Finally he said bruskly:

"And when did - did the change come to you?"

"In the carriage, when every turn of the wheel, every passing street, was rushing me away from you. I thought of you - alone - lost - and suddenly I knew. I beat with my fists on the window and called to the coachman like a madman. I don't know what I said. I came back."

She stopped, pressing back the tears that had started on her eyelids at the memory. She controlled herself, gave a quick little nod, without offering her hand, went toward the door.

"What! I've got to call her back!" He said it to himself, adding furiously: "Never!"

He let her go to the door itself, vowing he would not make the advance.

When the door was half open, something in him cried: "Wait!"

She closed the door softly, but she did not immediately turn round. The palms of her hands were wet with the cold, frightened sweat of that awful moment. When she returned, she came to him with a wondering, timid, girlish look in her eyes.

"Oh, Jack, if you only could!" she said, and then only did she put out her hands and let her fingers press over his heart.

The next moment she was swept up in his arms, shrinking and very still.

All at once he put her from him and said roughly:

"What was his name?"

"No, no!"

"Give me his name," he said miserably. "I must know it."

"No - neither now nor at any other time," she said firmly, and her look as it met his had again all the old domination. "That is my condition."

"Ah, how weak I have been," he said to himself, with a last bitter, instinctive revolt. "How weak I am."

She saw and understood.

"We must be generous," she said, changing her voice quickly to gentleness. "He has been pained enough already. He alone will suffer. And if you knew his name it would only make you unhappy."

He still rebelled, but suddenly to him came a thought which at first he was ashamed to express.

"He doesn't know?"

She lied.

"No."

"He's still waiting - there?"

"Yes."

"Ah, he's waiting," he said to himself.

A gleam of vanity, of triumph over the discarded, humiliated one, leaped up fiercely within him and ended all the lingering, bitter memories.

"Then you care?" she said, resting her head on his shoulder that he might not see she had read such a thought.

"Care?" he cried. He had surrendered. Now it was necessary to be convinced. "Why, when I received your letter I - I was wild. I wanted to do murder."

"Jackie!"

"I was like a madman - everything was gone - nothing was left."

"Oh, Jack, how I have made you suffer!"

"Suffer? Yes, I have suffered!" Overcome by the returning pain of the memory, he dropped into a chair, trying to control his voice. "Yes, I have suffered!"

"Forgive me!" she said, slipping on her knees beside him, and burying her head in his lap.

"I was out of my head - I don't know what I did, what I said. It was as though a bomb had exploded. My life was wrecked, shattered - nothing left."

He felt the grief again, even more acutely. He suffered for what he had suffered.

"Jack, I never really could have *abandoned* you," she cried bitterly. She raised her eyes toward him and suddenly took notice of the time-tables that lay clutched in his hands. "Oh, you were going away!"

He nodded, incapable of speech.

"You were running away?"

"I was running away - to forget - to bury myself!"

"Oh, Jack!"

"There was nothing here. It was all a blank! I was running away - to bury myself!"

At the memory of that miserable hopeless moment, in which he had resolved on flight, the tears, no longer to be denied, came dripping down his cheeks.

THE LIE

I

For some time they had ceased to speak, too oppressed with the needless anguish of this their last night. At their feet the tiny shining windows of Etretat were dropping back into the night, as though sinking under the rise of that black, mysterious flood that came luminously from the obscure regions of the faint sky. Overhead, the swollen August stars had faded before the pale flush that, toward the lighthouse on the cliff, heralded the red rise of the moon.

He held himself a little apart, the better to seize every filmy detail of the strange woman who had come inexplicably into his life, watching the long, languorous arms stretched out into an impulsive clasp, the dramatic harmony of the body, the brooding head, the soft, half-revealed line of the neck. The troubling alchemy of the night, that before his eyes slowly mingled the earth with the sea and the sea with the sky, seemed less mysterious than this woman whose body was as immobile as the stillness in her soul.

All at once he felt in her, whom he had known as he had known no other, something unknown, the coming of another woman, belonging to another life, the life of the opera and the multitude, which would again flatter and intoxicate her. The summer had passed without a doubt, and now, all at once, something new came to him, indefinable, colored with the vague terror of the night, the fear of other men who would come thronging about her, in the other life, where he could not follow.

Around the forked promontory to the east, the lights of the little packet-boat for England appeared, like the red cinder in a pipe, slipping toward the horizon. It was the signal for a lover's embrace, conceived long ago in fancy and kept in tenderness.

"Madeleine," he said, touching her arm. "There it is - our little boat."

"Ah! *le p'tit bateau* - with its funny red and green eyes."

She turned and raised her lips to his; and the kiss, which she did not give but permitted, seemed only fraught with an ineffable sadness, the end of all things, the tearing asunder and the numbness of separation. She returned to her pose, her eyes fixed on the little packet, saying:

"It's late."

"Yes."

"It goes fast."

"Very."

They spoke mechanically, and then not at all. The dread of the morning was too poignant to approach the

Owen Johnson

things that must be said. Suddenly, with the savage directness of the male to plunge into the pain which must be undergone, he began:

"It was like poison - that kiss."

She turned, forgetting her own anguish in the pain in his voice, murmuring, "Ben, my poor Ben."

"So you will go - to-morrow," he said bitterly, "back to the great public that will possess you, and I shall remain - here, alone."

"It must be so."

He felt suddenly an impulse he had not felt before, an instinct to make her suffer a little. He said brutally:

"But you want to go!"

She did not answer, but, in the obscurity, he knew her large eyes were searching his face. He felt ashamed of what he had said, and yet because she made no protestation, he persisted:

"You have left off your jewels, those jewels you can't do without."

"Not to-night."

"You who are never happy without them - why not to-night?"

As, carried away by the jealousy of what lay beyond, he was about to continue, she laid her fingers on his lips, with a little brusk, nervous movement of her shoulders.

"Don't - you don't understand."

But he understood and he resented the fact that she should have put aside the long undulating rope of pearls, the rings of rubies and emeralds that seemed as natural to her dark beauty as the roses to the spring. He had tried to understand her woman's nature, to believe that no memory yet lingered about them, to accept without question what had never belonged longed to their life together, and remembering what he had fought down he thought bitterly:

"She has changed me more than I have changed her. It is always so."

She moved a little, her pose, with instinctive dramatic sense, changing with her changing mood.

"Do not think I don't understand you," she said quietly.

"What do you understand?"

"It hurts you because I wish to return."

"That is not so, Madeleine," he said abruptly. "You know what big things I want you to do."

"I know - only you would like me to say the contrary - to protest that I would give it all up - be content to be with you alone."

"No, not that," he said grudgingly, "and yet, this last night - here - I should like to hear you say the contrary."

Owen Johnson

She laughed a low laugh and caught his hand a little tighter.

"That displeases you?"

"No, no, of course not!" Presently she added with an effort:

"There is so much that we must say to each other and we have not the courage."

"True, all summer we have never talked of what must come after."

"I want you to understand why I go back to it all, why I wish every year to be separated from you - yes, exactly, from you," she added, as his fingers contracted with an involuntary movement. "Ben, what has come to me I never expected would come. I love, but neither that word nor any other word can express how absolutely I have become yours. When I told you my life, you did not wonder how difficult it was for me to believe that such a thing could be possible. But you convinced me, and what has come to me has come as a miracle. I adore you. All my life has been lived just for this great love; ah yes, that's what I believe, what I feel." She leaned swiftly to him and allowed him to catch her to him in his strong arms. Then slowly disengaging herself, she continued, "You are a little hurt because I do not cry out what you would not accept, because I do not say that I would give up everything if you asked it."

"It is only to *hear* it," he said impulsively.

"But I have often wished it myself," she said slowly.

"There's not a day that I have not wished it - to give up everything and stay by you. Do you know why? From the longing that's in me now, the first unselfish longing I have ever had - to sacrifice myself for you in some way, somehow. It is more than a hunger, it is a need of the soul - of my love itself. It comes over me sometimes as tears come to my eyes when you are away, and I say to myself, 'I love him,' and yet, Ben, I shall not, I shall never give up my career, not now, not for years to come."

"No," he said mechanically.

"We are two great idealists, for that is what you have made me, Ben. Before I was always laughing, and I believed in nothing. I despised even what my sacrifice had won. Now, when I am with you, I remain in a revery, and I am happy - happy with the happiness of things I cannot understand. To-night, by your side, it seems to me I have never felt the night before or known the mystery of the silent, faint hours. You have made me feel the loneliness of the human soul, and that impulse it must have before these things that are beyond us, that surround us, dominate us, to cling almost in terror to another soul. You have so completely made me over that it is as though you had created me yourself. I am thirty-five. I have known everything else but what you have awakened in me, and because I have this knowledge and this hunger I can see clearer what we must do. You and I are a little romanesque, but remember that even a great love may tire and grow stale, and that is what I won't have, what must not be." Her voice had risen with the intensity of her mood. She said more solemnly: "You are afraid of other men, of other moods of mine - you have no reason. This love which comes to some as the awakening of life is to me the end of all things. If anything should wound it or belittle it, I should not survive it."

She continued to speak, in a low unvarying voice. He felt his mind clear and his doubts dissipate, and impatiently he waited for her to end, to show her that his weakness of the moment was gone and that he was still the man of big vision who had awakened her.

"There are people who can put in order their love as they put in order their house. We are not of that kind, Ben. I am a woman who has lived on sensations. You, too, are a dreamer and a poet at the bottom. If I should give up the opera and become to you simply a housewife, if there was no longer any difficulty in our having each other, you would still love me - yes, because you are loyal - but the romanticism, the mystery, the longing we both need would vanish. Oh, I know. Well, you and I, we are the same. We can only live on a great passion, and to have fierce, unutterable joys we must suffer also - the suffering of separation. Do you understand?"

"Yes, I do."

"That is why I shall never give up my career. That is why I can bear the sadness of leaving you. I want you to be proud of me, Ben. I want you to think of me as some one whom thousands desire and only you can have. I want our love to be so intense that every day spent apart is heavy with the longing for each other; every day together precious because it will be a day nearer the awful coming of another separation. Believe me, I am right. I have thought much about it. You have your diplomatic career and your ambitions. You are proud. I have never asked you to give that up to follow me. I would not insult you. In January you will have a leave of absence, and we will be together for a few wonderful weeks, and in May I shall return here. Nothing will be changed." She extended her arm to where a faint red point still showed on the unseen water. "And each night we will wait, as we have waited, side by side, the coming of our little boat, - *notre p'tit bateau*"

"You are right," he said, placing his lips to her forehead. "I was jealous. I am sorry. It is over."

"But I, too, am jealous," she said, smiling.

"You?"

"Of course - no one can love without being jealous. Oh, I shall be afraid of every woman who comes near you. It will be an agony," she said, and the fire in her eyes brought him more healing happiness than all her words.

"You are right," he repeated.

He left her with a little pressure of the hand, and walked to the edge of the veranda. A nervous, sighing breeze had come with the full coming of the moon, and underneath him he heard the troubled rustle of leaves in the obscurity, the sifting and drifting of tired, loose things, the stir of the night which awakened a restless mood in his soul. He had listened to her as she had proclaimed her love, and yet this love, without illusions, sharply recalled to him other passions. He remembered his first love, a boy-and-girl affair, and sharply contrasting it with a sudden ache to this absence of impulse and illusions, of phrases, vows, without logic, thrown out in the sweet madness of the moment. Why had she not cried out something impulsive, promised things that could not be. Then he realized, standing there in the harvest moonlight, in the breaking up of summer, that he was no longer a youth, that certain things could not be lived over, and that, as she had said, he too felt that this was the great love, the last that he would share; that if it ended, his youth ended and with his youth all that in him clung to life.

He turned and saw her, chin in the flat of her palm, steadily following his mood. He had taken but a dozen steps, and yet he had placed a thousand miles between them. He had almost a feeling of treachery, and to dispel these new unquiet thoughts he repeated to himself again:

"She is right."

But he did not immediately return. The memory of other loves, faint as they had been in comparison with this all-absorbing impulse, had yet given him a certain objective point of view. He saw himself clearly, and he understood what of pain the future had in store for him.

"How I shall suffer!" he said to himself.

"You are going so far away from me," she said suddenly, warned by some woman's instinct.

He was startled at the conjunction of her words and his moods. He returned hastily, and sat down beside her. She took his head in her hands and looked anxiously into his eyes.

"What is it?" she said. "You are afraid?"

"A little," he said reluctantly.

"Of what - of the months that will come?"

"Of the past."

"What do you mean?" she said, withdrawing a little as though disturbed by the thought.

"When I am with you I know there is not a corner of your heart that I do not possess," he began evasively.

"Well?"

"Only it's the past - the habits of the past," he murmured. "I know you so well, Madeleine, you have need of strength, you don't go on alone. That is the genius of women like you - to reach out and attach to themselves men who will strengthen them, compel them on."

"Ah, I understand," she said slowly.

"Yes, that is what I'm afraid of," he said rapidly.

"You are thinking of the artist, not the woman."

"Ah, there is no difference - not to a man who loves," he said impulsively. "I know how great your love is for me, and I believe in it. I know nothing will come to efface it. Only you will be lonely, you'll have your trials and annoyances, days of depression, of doubt, when you will need some one to restore your faith in yourself, your courage in your work, and then, I don't say you will love any one else, but you will need some one near you who loves you, always at your service - "

"If you could only understand me," she said, interrupting him. "Men, other men, are like actors to me. When I am on the stage, when I am playing Manon, do you think I see who is playing Des Grieux? Not at all. He is there, he gives me my *replique*, he excites my nerves, I say a thousand things under my breath, when I am in his arms I adore him, but when the curtain goes down, I go off the stage and don't even say good night to him."

"But he, he doesn't know that."

"Of course not; tenors never do. Well, that is just the way I have lived, that is just what men have meant to me. They give the *replique* to my moods, to my needs, and when I have no longer need of them, I go off tranquilly. That is all there is to it. I take from them what I want. Of course they will be around me, but they will be nothing to me. They will be like managers, press-agents, actors. Don't you understand that?"

"Yes, yes, I understand," he said without sincerity. Then he blurted out, "I wish you had not said it, all the same."

"Why?"

"I cannot see it as you see it, and besides, you put a doubt in my mind that I never wish to feel."

"What doubt?"

"Do I really have you, or only a mood of yours?"

"Ben!"

"I know. I know. No, I am not going to think such things. That would be unworthy of what we have felt." He paused a moment, and when he spoke again his voice was under control. "Madeleine, remember well what I say to you now. I shall probably never again speak to you with such absolute truth, or even acknowledge it to myself. I accept the necessity of separation. I know all the sufferings it will bring, all the doubts, the unreasoning jealousies. I am big enough in experience to understand what you have just suggested to me, but as a man who loves you, Madeleine, I will never understand it. I know that a dozen men may come into your life, interest you intensely, even absorb you for a while, and that they would still mean nothing to you the moment I come. Well, I am different. A man is different. While you are away, I shall not see a woman without resentment; I shall not think of any one but you, and if I did, I would cease to love you."

"But why?"

"Because I cannot share anything of what belongs to you. That is my nature. There is no use in pretending the contrary. Yours is different, and I understand why it is so. I have listened to many confidences, understood many lives that others would not understand. I have always maintained that it is the natural thing for a human being to love many times - even that there might he in the same heart a great, overpowering love and a little one. I still believe it - with my mind. I know it is so. These are the things we like to analyze in human nature together. I know it is true, but it is not true for me. No, I would never understand it in you. I know myself too well, I am jealous of everything of the past - oh, insanely jealous. I know that no sooner are you gone than I will be tortured by the most ridiculous doubts. I will see you in the moonlight all across that endless sea with other men near you. I will dream of other men with millions, ready to give you everything your eyes adore. I will imagine men of big minds that will fascinate you. I will even say to myself that now that you have known what a great love can mean you will all the more be likely to need it, to seek something to counterfeit it - "

"Ben, my poor Ben - frightful," she murmured.

"That is how it is. Shall I tell you something else?"

"What?"

"I wish devoutly you had never told me a word of - of the past."

"But how can you say such things? We have been honest with each other. You yourself - "

"I know, I know, I have no right myself, and yet there it is. It is something fearful, this madness of possession that comes to me. No, I have no fear that I will not always be first in your heart, only I understand the needs, the habits, of your nature. I understand myself now as I have not before, and that's why I say to you solemnly, Madeleine, if ever for a moment another man should come into your life - never, never, let me know."

"But - "

"No, don't say anything that I may remember to torture me. Lie to me."

"I have never lied."

"Madeleine, it is better to be merciful than to tell the truth, and, after all, what does such a confession mean? It only means that you free your conscience and that the wound - the ache - remains with the other. Whatever happens, never tell me. Do you understand?"

This time she made no answer. She even ceased to look at him, her head dropped back, her arms motionless, one finger only revolving slowly on the undulating arm of her chair.

"I shall try by all the strength that is in me never to ask that question," he rushed on. "I know I shall make a hundred vows not to do so, and I know that the first time I look into your face I shall blurt it out. Ah, if - if - if it must be so, never let me know, for there are thoughts I cannot bear now that I've known you." He flung himself at her side and took her roughly in his arms. "Madeleine, I know what I am saying. I may tell you the contrary later. I may say it lightly, pretending it is of no importance. I may beg the truth of you with tears in my eyes - I may swear to you that nothing but honesty counts between us, that I can understand, forgive, forget everything. Well, whatever I say or do, never, never let me know - if you value my happiness, my peace of mind, my life even!"

She laid her hand on his lips and then on his forehead to calm him, drawing his head to her shoulder.

"Listen, Ben," she said, gently. "I, the Madeleine Conti who loves you, am another being. I adore you so that I shall hate all other men, as you will hate all other women. There will never be the slightest deceit or infidelity between us. Ask any questions of me at any time. I know there can be from now on but one answer. Have no fear. Do not tire yourself in a senseless fever. There is so little time left. I love you."

Never had he heard her voice so deep with sincerity and tenderness, and yet, as he surrendered to the touch of her soft hands, yielding up all his doubts, he was conscious of a new alarm creeping into his heart; and, dissatisfied with what he himself had a moment before implored, in the breath with which he whispered, "I believe you," he said to himself:

"Does she say that because she believes it or has she begun to lie?"

II

For seven years they lived the same existence, separated sometimes for three months, occasionally for six, and once because of a trip taken to South America for nearly a year.

The first time that he joined her, after five months of longing, he remained a week without crying out the words that were heavy on his heart. One day she said to him:

"What is there - back of your eyes, hidden away, that you are stifling?"

"You know," he blurted out.

"What?"

"Ah, I have tried not to say it, to live it down. I can't - it's beyond me. I shall have no peace until it is said."

"Then say it."

He took her face in his two hands and looked into her eyes.

"Since I have been away," he said brutally, "there has been no one else in your heart? You have been true to

Owen Johnson

me, to our love?"

"I have been true," she answered with a little smile.

He held his eyes on hers a long while, hesitating whether to be silent or to continue, and then, all at once, convinced, burst into tears and begged her pardon.

"Oh, I shouldn't have asked it - forgive me."

"Do whatever is easiest for you, my love," she answered. "There is nothing to forgive. I understand all. I love you for it."

Only she never asked him any questions, and that alarmed him.

The second time report had coupled her name with a Gabriel Lombardi, a great baritone with whom she was appearing. When he arrived, as soon as they were alone, he swung her about in his arms and cried in a strangled voice:

"Swear to me that you have been faithful."

"I swear."

"Gabriel Lombardi"?

"I can't abide him".

"Ah, if I had never told you to lie to me - fool that I was."

Then she said calmly, with that deep conviction which

always moved him: "Ben, when you asked me that, I told you I would never lie. I have told you the truth. No man has ever had the pressure of my fingers, and no man ever will."

So intense had been his emotion that he had almost a paroxysm. When he opened his eyes he found her face wet with tears.

"Ah, Madeleine," he said, "I am brutal with you. I cannot help it."

"I would not have you love me differently," she said gently, and through her tears he seemed to see a faint, elusive smile, that was gone quickly if it was ever there at all.

Another time, he said to himself: "No, I will say nothing. She will come to me herself, put her arms around me, and tell me with a smile that no other thought has been in her heart all this while. That's it. If I wait she will make the move, she will make the move each time - and that will be much better."

He waited three days, but she made no allusion. He waited another, and then he said lightly:

"You see, I am reforming."

"How so?"

"Why, I don't ask foolish questions any more."

"That's so."

"Still - "

"Well?" she said, looking up.

"Still, you might have guessed what I wanted," he answered, a little hurt.

She rose quickly and came lightly to him, putting her hand on his shoulder.

"Is that what you wish?" she said.

"Yes."

She repeated slowly her protestations and when she had ended, said, "Take me in your arms - hurt me."

"Now she will understand," he thought; "the next time she will not wait."

But each time, though he martyrized his soul in patience, he was forced to bring up the question that would not let him rest.

He could not understand why she did not save him this useless agony. Sometimes when he wanted to find an excuse he said to himself it was because she felt humiliated that he should still doubt. At other times, he stumbled on explanations that terrified him. Then he remembered with bitterness the promise that he had exacted from her, a promise that, instead of bringing him peace, had left only an endless torment, and forgetting all his protestations he would cry to himself, in a cold perspiration:

"Ah, if she is really lying, how can I ever be sure?"

III

In the eighth year, Madeleine Conti retired from the stage and announced her marriage. After five years of complete happiness she was taken suddenly ill, as the result of exposure to a drenching storm. One afternoon, as he waited by her bedside, talking in broken tones of all that they had been to each other, he said to her in a voice that he tried nervously to school to quietness:

"Madeleine, you know that our life together has been without the slightest shadow from the first. You know we have proved to each other how immense our love has been. In all these years I have grown in maturity and understanding. I regret only one thing, and I have regretted it bitterly, every day - that I once asked you, if - if ever for a moment another man came into your life to hide it from me, to tell me a lie. It was a great mistake. I have never ceased to regret it. Our love has been so above all worldly things that there ought not to be the slightest concealment between us. I release you from that promise. Tell me now the truth. It will mean nothing to me. During the eight years when we were separated there were - there must have been times, times of loneliness, of weakness, when other men came into your life. Weren't there?"

She turned and looked at him steadily, her large eyes seeming larger and more brilliant from the heightened fever of her cheeks. Then she made a little negative sign of her head, still looking at him.

"No, never."

"You don't understand, Madeleine," he said, dissatisfied, "or you are still thinking of what I said to you there in Etretat. That was thirteen years ago. Then I had just begun to love you, I feared for the future, for everything. Now I have tested you, and I have never had a doubt. I know the difference between the flesh and the spirit. I know your two selves; I know how impossible it would have been otherwise. Now you can tell me."

"There is nothing - to tell," she said slowly.

"I expected that you would have other men who loved you about you," he said, feverishly. "I knew it would be so. I swear to you I expected it. I know why you continue to deny it. It's for my sake, isn't it? I love you for it. But, believe me, in such a moment there ought nothing to stand between us. Madeleine, Madeleine, I beg you, tell me the truth."

She continued to gaze at him fixedly, without turning away her great eyes, as forgetting himself, he rushed on:

"Yes, let me know the truth - that will be nothing now. Besides, I have guessed it. Only I must know one way or the other. All these years I have lived in doubt. You see what it means to me. You must understand what is due me after all our life together. Madeleine, did you lie to me?"

"No."

"Listen," he said, desperately. "You never asked me the same question - why, I never understood - but if you had questioned me I could not have answered truthfully what you did. There, you see, there is no longer the slightest reason why you should not speak the truth."

She half closed her eyes - wearily.

"I have told - the truth."

"Ah, I can't believe it," he cried, carried away. "Oh, cursed day when I told you what I did. It's that which tortures me. You adore me - you don't wish to hurt me, to leave a wound behind, but I swear to you if you told me the truth I should feel a great weight taken from my heart, a weight that has been here all these years. I should know that every corner of your soul had been shown to me, nothing withheld. I should know absolutely, Madeleine, believe me, when I tell you this, when I tell you I must know. Every day of my life I have paid the penalty, I have suffered the doubts of the damned, I have never known an hour's peace! I beg you, I implore you, only let me know the truth; the truth - I must know the truth!"

He stopped suddenly, trembling all over, and held out his hands to her, his face lashed with suffering.

"I have not lied," she said slowly, after a long study. She raised her eyes, feebly made the sign of the cross, and whispered, "I swear it."

Then he no longer held in his tears. He dropped his

head, and his body shook with sobs, while from time to time he repeated, "Thank God, thank God."

IV

The next day Madeleine Conti had a sudden turn for the worse, which surprised the attendants. Doctor Kimball, the American, doctor, and Pere Francois, who had administered the last rites, were walking together in the little formal garden, where the sun flung short, brilliant shadows of scattered foliage about them.

"She was an extraordinary artist and her life was more extraordinary," said Dr. Kimball. "I heard her debut at the Opera Comique. For ten years her name was the gossip of all Europe. Then all at once she meets a man whom no one knows, falls in love, and is transformed. These women are really extraordinary examples of hysteria. Each time I know one it makes me understand the scientific phenomenon of Mary Magdalene. It is really a case of nerve reaction. The moral fever that is the fiercest burns itself out the quickest and seems to leave no trace behind. In this case love came also as a religious conversion. I should say the phenomena were identical."

"She was happy," said the cure, turning to go.

"Yes, it was a great romance."

"A rare one. She adored him. Love is a tide that cleanses all."

"Yet she was of the stage up to the last. You know she would not have her husband in the room at the end."

"She had a great heart," said the cure quietly. "She wished to spare him that suffering."

"She had an extraordinary will," said the doctor, glancing at him quickly. He added, tentatively: "She asked two questions that were curious enough."

"Indeed," said the cure, lingering a moment with his hand on the gate.

"She wanted to know whether persons in a delirium talked of the past and if after death the face returned to its calm."

"What did you say to her about the effects of delirium?" said the cure with his blank face.

"That it was a point difficult to decide," said the doctor slowly. "Undoubtedly, in a delirium, everything is mixed, the real and the imagined, the memory and the fantasy, actual experience and the inner dream-life of the mind which is so difficult to classify. It was after that, that she made her husband promise to see her only when she was conscious and to remain away at the last."

"It is easily understood," said the cure quietly, without change of expression on his face that held the secrets of a thousand confessionals. "As you say, for ten years she had lived a different life. She was afraid that in her delirium some reference to that time might wound unnecessarily the man who had made over her life. She had a great courage. Peace be with her soul."

"Still," - Doctor Kimball hesitated, as though considering the phrasing of a delicate question; but Father Francois, making a little amical sign of adieu, passed out of the garden, and for a moment his blank face was illumined by one of those rare smiles, such as one sees on the faces of holy men; smiles that seem in perfect faith to look upon the mysteries of the world to come.

EVEN THREES

I

Ever since the historic day when a visiting clergyman accomplished the feat of pulling a ball from the tenth tee at an angle of two hundred and twenty-five degrees into the river that is the rightful receptacle for the eighth tee, the Stockbridge golf-course has had seventeen out of theeighteen holes that are punctuated with possible water hazards. The charming course itself lies in the flat of the sunken meadows which the Housatonic, in the few thousand years which are necessary for the proper preparation of a golf-course, has obligingly eaten out of the high, accompanying bluffs. The river, which goes wriggling on its way as though convulsed with merriment, is garnished with luxurious elms and willows, which occasionally deflect to the difficult putting-greens the random slices of certain notorious amateurs.

From the spectacular bluffs of the educated village of Stockbridge nothing can be imagined more charming than the panorama that the course presents on a busy day. Across the soft, green stretches, diminutive caddies may be seen scampering with long buckling-nets, while from the river-banks numerous recklessly exposed legs wave in the air as the more socially presentable portions hang frantically over the swirling current. Occasionally an enthusiastic golfer, driving from the eighth or ninth tees, may be seen to start immediately in headlong pursuit of a diverted ball, the swing of the club and the intuitive leap of the legs forward forming so continuous a movement that the main purpose of the game often becomes obscured to the mere spectator. Nearer, in the numerous languid swales that nature has generously provided to protect the interests of the manufacturers, or in the rippling patches of unmown grass, that in the later hours will be populated by enthusiastic caddies, desperate groups linger in botanizing attitudes.

Every morning lawyers who are neglecting their clients, doctors who have forgotten their patients, business men who have sacrificed their affairs, even ministers of the gospel who have forsaken their churches, gather in the noisy dressing-room and listen with servile attention while some unscrubbed boy who goes around under eighty imparts a little of his miraculous knowledge.

Two hours later, for every ten that have gone out so blithely, two return crushed and despondent, denouncing and renouncing the game, once and for all, absolutely and finally, until the afternoon, when they return like thieves in the night and venture out in a desperate hope; two more come stamping back in even more offensive enthusiasm; and the remainder straggle home moody and disillusioned, reviving their sunken spirits by impossible tales of past accomplishments.

There is something about these twilight gatherings that suggests the degeneracy of a rugged race; nor is the contamination of merely local significance. There are those who lie consciously, with a certain frank,

Owen Johnson

commendable, whole-hearted plunge into iniquity. Such men return to their worldly callings with intellectual vigor unimpaired and a natural reaction toward the decalogue. Others of more casuistical temperament, unable all at once to throw over the traditions of a New England conscience to the exigencies of the game, do not burst at once into falsehood, but by a confusing process weaken their memories and corrupt their imaginations. They never lie of the events of the day. Rather they return to some jumbled happening of the week before and delude themselves with only a lingering qualm, until from habit they can create what is really a form of paranoia, the delusion of greatness, or the exaggerated ego. Such men, inoculated with self-deception, return to the outer world, to deceive others, lower the standards of business morality, contaminate politics, and threaten the vigor of the republic. R.N. Booverman, the Treasurer, and Theobald Pickings, the unenvied Secretary of an unenvied hoard, arrived at the first tee at precisely ten o'clock on a certain favorable morning in early August to begin the thirty-six holes which six times a week, six months of the year, they played together as sympathetic and well-matched adversaries. Their intimacy had arisen primarily from the fact that Pickings was the only man willing to listen to Booverman's restless dissertations on the malignant fates which seemed to pursue him even to the neglect of their international duties, while Booverman, in fair exchange, suffered Pickings to enlarge ad libitum on his theory of the rolling versus the flat putting-greens.

Pickings was one of those correctly fashioned and punctilious golfers whose stance was modeled on classic lines, whose drive, though it averaged only twenty-five yards over the hundred, was always a well-oiled and graceful exhibition of the Royal St. Andrew's swing, the left sole thrown up, the eyeballs bulging with the last muscular tension, the club carried back until the whole body was contorted into the first position of the traditional hoop-snake preparing to descend a hill. He used the interlocking grip, carried a bag with a spoon driver, an aluminium cleek, three abnormal putters, and wore one chamois glove with air-holes on the back. He never accomplished the course in less than eighty five and never exceeded ninety four, but, having aimed to set a correct example rather than to strive vulgarly for professional records, was always in a state of offensive optimism due to a complete sartorial satisfaction.

Booverman, on the contrary, had been hailed in his first years as a coming champion. With three holes eliminated, he could turn in a card distinguished for its fours and threes; but unfortunately these sad lapses inevitably occurred. As Booverman himself admitted, his appearance on the golf-links was the signal for the capricious imps of chance who stir up politicians to indiscreet truths and keep the Balkan pot of discord bubbling, to forsake immediately these prime duties, and enjoy a little relaxation at his expense.

Now, for the first three years Booverman responded in a manner to delight imp and devil. When standing thirty-four for the first six holes, he sliced into the jungle, and, after twenty minutes of frantic beating of the bush, was forced to acknowledge a lost ball and no score, he promptly sat down, tore large clutches of grass from the sod, and expressed himself to the admiring delight of the caddies, who favorably compared his flow of impulsive expletives to the choice moments of their own home life. At other times

Owen Johnson

he would take an offending club firmly in his big hands and break it into four pieces, which he would drive into the ground, hurling the head itself, with a last diabolical gesture, into the Housatonic River, which, as may be repeated, wriggles its way through the course as though convulsed with merriment.

There were certain trees into which he inevitably drove, certain waggish bends of the river where, no matter how he might face, he was sure to arrive. There was a space of exactly ten inches under the clubhouse where his balls alone could disappear. He never ran down a long put, but always hung on the rim of the cup. It was his adversary who executed phenomenal shots, approaches of eighty yards that dribbled home, sliced drives that hit a fence and bounded back on the course. Nothing of this agreeable sort had ever happened or could ever happen to him. Finally the conviction of a certain predestined damnation settled upon him. He no longer struggled; his once rollicking spirits settled into a moody despair. Nothing encouraged him or could trick him into a display of hope. If he achieved a four and two twos on the first holes, he would say vindictively:

"What's the use? I'll lose my ball on the fifth."

And when this happened, he no longer swore, but said gloomily with even a sense of satisfaction: "You can't get me excited. Didn't I know it would happen?"

Once in a while he had broken out, "If ever my luck changes, if it comes all at once - "

But he never ended the sentence, ashamed, as it were, to have indulged in such a childish fancy. Yet, as

Providence moves in a mysterious way its wonders to perform, it was just this invincible pessimism that alone could have permitted Booverman to accomplish the incredible experience that befell him.

II

Topics of engrossing mental interests are bad form on the golf-links, since they leave a disturbing memory in the mind to divert it from that absolute intellectual concentration which the game demands. Therefore Pickings and Booverman, as they started toward the crowded first tee, remarked *de rigueur*:

"Good weather."

"A bit of a breeze."

"Not strong enough to affect the drives."

"The greens have baked out."

"Fast as I've seen them."

"Well, it won't help me."

"How do you know?" said Pickings, politely, for the hundredth time. "Perhaps this is the day you'll get your score."

Booverman ignored this set remark, laying his ball on the rack, where two predecessors were waiting, and settled beside Pickings at the foot of the elm which later, he knew, would rob him of a four on the home green.

Wessels and Pollock, literary representatives, were preparing to drive. They were converts of the summer, each sacrificing their season's output in a frantic effort to surpass the other. Pickings, the purist, did not approve of them in the least. They brought to the royal and ancient game a spirit of Bohemian irreverence and banter that offended his serious enthusiasm.

When Wessels made a convulsive stab at his ball and luckily achieved good distance, Pollock remarked behind his hand, "A good shot, damn it!"

Wessels stationed himself in a hopefully deprecatory attitude and watched Pollock build a monument of sand, balance his ball, and whistling nervously through his teeth, lunge successfully down. Whereupon, in defiance of etiquette, he swore with equal fervor, and they started off.

Pickings glanced at Booverman in a superior and critical way, but at this moment a thin, dyspeptic man with undisciplined whiskers broke in serenely without waiting for the answers to the questions he propounded:

"Ideal weather, eh? Came over from Norfolk this morning; ran over at fifty miles an hour. Some going, eh? They tell me you've quite a course here; record around seventy-one, isn't it? Good deal of water to keep out of? You gentlemen some of the cracks? Course pretty fast with all this dry weather? What do you think of the one-piece driver? My friend, Judge Weatherup. My name's Yancy - Cyrus P."

Owen Johnson

A ponderous person who looked as though he had been pumped up for the journey gravely saluted, while his feverish companion rolled on:

"Your course's rather short, isn't it? Imagine it's rather easy for a straight driver. What's your record? Seventy-one amateur? Rather high, isn't it? Do you get many cracks around here? Caddies seem scarce. Did either of you gentlemen ever reflect how surprising it is that better scores aren't made at this game? Now, take seventy-one; that's only one under fours, and I venture to say at least six of your holes are possible twos, and all the rest, sometime or other, have been made in three. Yet you never hear of phenomenal scores, do you, like a run of luck at roulette or poker? You get my idea?"

"I believe it is your turn, sir," said Pickings, both crushing and parliamentary. "There are several waiting."

Judge Weatherup drove a perfect ball into the long grass, where successful searches averaged ten minutes, while his voluble companion, with an immense expenditure of force, foozled into the swale to the left, which was both damp and retentive.

"Shall we play through?" said Pickings, with formal preciseness. He teed his ball, took exactly eight full practice swings, and drove one hundred and fifty yards as usual directly in the middle of the course.

"Well, it's straight; that's all can be said for it," he said, as he would say at the next seventeen tees.

Booverman rarely employed that slogan. That straight

and narrow path was not in his religious practice. He drove a long ball, and he drove a great many that did not return in his bag. He glanced resentfully to the right, where Judge Weatherup was straddling the fence, and to the left, where Yancy was annoying the bullfrogs.

"Darn them!" he said to himself. "Of course now I'll follow suit."

But whether or not the malignant force of suggestion was neutralized by the attraction in opposite directions, his drive went straight and far, a beautiful two hundred and forty yards.

"Tine shot, Mr. Booverman," said Frank, the professional, nodding his head, "free and easy, plenty of follow-through."

"You're on your drive to-day," said Pickings, cheerfully.

"Sure! When I get a good drive off the first tee," said Booverman discouraged, "I mess up all the rest. You'll see."

"Oh, come now," said Pickings, as a matter of form. He played his shot, which came methodically to the edge of the green.

Booverman took his mashy for the short running-up stroke to the pin, which seemed so near.

"I suppose I've tried this shot a thousand times," he said savagely. "Any one else would get a three once in five times - any one but Jonah's favorite brother."

He swung carelessly, and watched with a tolerant interest the white ball roll on to the green straight for the flag. All at once Wessels and Pollock, who were ahead, sprang into the air and began agitating their hats.

"By George! it's in!" said Pickings. "You've run it down. First hole in two! Well, what do you think of that?"

Booverman, unconvinced, approached the hole with suspicion, gingerly removing the pin. At the bottom, sure enough, lay his ball for a phenomenal two.

"That's the first bit of luck that has ever happened to me," he said furiously; "absolutely the first time in my whole career."

"I say, old man," said Pickings, in remonstrance, "you're not angry about it, are you?"

"Well, I don't know whether I am or not," said Booverman, obstinately. In fact, he felt rather defrauded. The integrity of his record was attacked. "See here, I play thirty-six holes a day, two hundred and sixteen a week, a thousand a month, six thousand a year; ten years, sixty thousand holes; and this is the first time a bit of luck has ever happened to me - once in sixty thousand times."

Pickings drew out a handkerchief and wiped his forehead.

"It may come all at once," he said faintly.

This mild hope only infuriated Booverman. He had

already teed his ball for the second hole, which was poised on a rolling hill one hundred and thirty-five yards away. It is considered rather easy as golf-holes go. The only dangers are a matted wilderness of long grass in front of the tee, the certainty of landing out of bounds on the slightest slice, or of rolling down hill into a soggy substance on a pull. Also there is a tree to be hit and a sand-pit to be sampled.

"Now watch my little friend the apple-tree," said Booverman. "I'm going to play for it, because, if I slice, I lose my ball, and that knocks my whole game higher than a kite." He added between his teeth: "All I ask is to get around to the eighth hole before I lose my ball. I know I'll lose it there."

Due to the fact that his two on the first brought him not the slightest thrill of nervous joy, he made a perfect shot, the ball carrying the green straight and true.

"This is your day all right," said Pickings, stepping to the tee.

"Oh, there's never been anything the matter with my irons," said Booverman, darkly. "Just wait till we strike the fourth and fifth holes."

When they climbed the hill, Booverman's ball lay within three feet of the cup, which he easily putted out.

"Two down," said Pickings, inaudibly. "By George! what a glorious start!"

"Once in sixty thousand times," said Booverman to himself. The third hole lay two hundred and five yards below, backed by the road and trapped by ditches, where at that moment Pollock, true to his traditions as a war correspondent, was laboring in the trenches, to the unrestrained delight of Wessels, who had passed beyond.

"Theobald," said Booverman, selecting his cleek and speaking with inspired conviction, "I will tell you exactly what is going to happen. I will smite this little homeopathic pill, and it will land just where I want it. I will probably put out for another two. Three holes in twos would probably excite any other human being on the face of this globe. It doesn't excite me. I know too well what will follow on the fourth or fifth. Watch."

"Straight to the pin," said Pickings in a loud whisper. "You've got a dead line on every shot to-day. Marvelous! When you get one of your streaks, there's certainly no use in my playing."

"Streak's the word," said Booverman, with a short, barking laugh. "Thank heaven, though, Pickings, I know it! Five years ago I'd have been shaking like a leaf. Now it only disgusts me. I've been fooled too often; I don't bite again."

In this same profoundly melancholic mood he approached his ball, which lay on the green, hole high, and put down a difficult put, a good three yards for his third two.

Pickings, despite all his classic conservatism, was so overcome with excitement that he twice putted over the hole for a shameful five.

Booverman's face as he walked to the fourth tee was as joyless as a London fog. He placed his ball carelessly, selected his driver, and turned on the fidgety Pickings with the gloomy solemnity of a father about to indulge in corporal punishment.

"Once in sixty thousand times, Picky. Do you realize what a start like this - three twos - would mean to a professional like Frank or even an amateur that hadn't offended every busy little fate and fury in the whole hoodooing business? Why, the blooming record would be knocked into the middle of next week."

"You'll do it," said Pickings in a loud whisper. "Play carefully."

Booverman glanced down the four-hundred-yard straightaway and murmured to himself:

"I wonder, little ball, whither will you fly?
I wonder, little ball, have I bid you good-by?
Will it be 'mid the prairies in the regions to the west?
Will it be in the marshes where the pollywogs nest?
Oh, tell me, little ball, is it ta-ta or good-by?"

He pronounced the last word with a settled conviction, and drove another long, straight drive. Pickings, thrilled at the possibility of another miracle, sliced badly.

"This is one of the most truly delightful holes of a picturesque course," said Booverman, taking out an approaching cleek for his second shot. "Nothing is more artistic than the tiny little patch of putting-green under the shaggy branches of the willows. The receptive graveyard to the right gives a certain pathos to it, a splendid, quiet note in contrast to the feeling of the swift, hungry river to the left, which will now receive and carry from my outstretched hand this little white floater that will float away from me. No matter; I say again the fourth green is a thing of ravishing beauty."

This second shot, low and long, rolled up in the same unvarying line.

"On the green," said Pickings.

"Short," said Booverman, who found, to his satisfaction, that he was right by a yard.

"Take your time," said Pickings, biting his nails.

"Rats! I'll play it for a five," said Booverman.

His approach ran up on the line, caught the rim of the cup, hesitated, and passed on a couple of feet.

"A four, anyway," said Pickings, with relief.

"I should have had a three," said Booverman, doggedly. "Any one else would have had a three, straight on the cup. You'd have had a three, Picky; you know you would."

Pickings did not answer. He was slowly going to pieces, forgetting the invincible stoicism that is the pride of the true golfer.

"I say, take your time, old chap," he said, his voice no longer under control. "Go slow! go slow!"

"Picky, for the first four years I played this course," said Booverman, angrily, "I never got better than a six on this simple three-hundred-and-fifty-yard hole. I lost my ball five times out of seven. There is something irresistibly alluring to me in the mosquito patches to my right. I think it is the fond hope that when I lose this nice new ball I may step inadvertently on one of its hundred brothers, which I may then bring home and give decent burial."

Pickings, who felt a mad and ungolfish desire to entreat him to caution, walked away to fight down his emotion.

"Well?" he said, after the click of the club had sounded.

"Well," said Booverman, without joy, "that ball is lying about two hundred and forty yards straight up the course, and by this time it has come quietly to a little cozy home in a nice, deep hoof track, just as I found it yesterday afternoon. Then I will have the exquisite pleasure of taking my niblick, and whanging it out for the loss of a stroke. That'll infuriate me, and I'll slice or pull. The best thing to do, I suppose, would be to play for a conservative six."

When, after four butchered shots, Pickings had advanced to where Booverman had driven, the ball lay in clear position just beyond the bumps and rills that ordinarily welcome a long shot. Booverman played a perfect mashy, which dropped clear on the green, and ran down a moderate put for a three.

They then crossed the road and arrived by a planked walk at a dirt mound in the midst of a swamp. Before them the cozy marsh lay stagnant ahead and then sloped to the right in the figure of a boomerang, making for those who fancied a slice a delightful little carry of one hundred and fifty yards. To the left was a procession of trees, while beyond, on the course, for those who drove a long ball, a giant willow had fallen the year before in order to add a new perplexity and foster the enthusiasm for luxury that was beginning among the caddies.

"I have a feeling," said Booverman, as though puzzled but not duped by what had happened - "I have a strange feeling that I'm not going to get into trouble here. That would be too obvious. It's at the seventh or eighth holes that something is lurking around for me. Well, I won't waste time."

He slapped down his ball, took a full swing, and carried the far-off bank with a low, shooting drive that continued bounding on.

"That ought to roll forever," said Pickings, red with excitement.

"The course is fast - dry as a rock," said Booverman, deprecatingly.

Pickings put three balls precisely into the bubbling water, and drew alongside on his eighth shot. Boover-man's drive had skimmed over the dried plain for a fair two hundred and seventy-five yards. His second shot, a full brassy, rolled directly on the green.

"If he makes a four here," said Pickings to himself, "he'll be playing five under four - no, by thunder! seven under four!" Suddenly he stopped, over-whelmed. "Why, he's actually around threes - two under three now. Heavens! If he ever suspects it, he'll go into a thousand pieces."

As a result, he missed his own ball completely, and then topped it for a bare fifty yards.

"I've never seen you play so badly," said Booverman in a grumbling tone. "You'll end up by throwing me off."

When they arrived at the green, Booverman's ball lay about thirty feet from the flag.

"It's a four, a sure four," said Pickings under his breath.

Suddenly Booverman burst into an exclamation.

"Picky, come here. Look - look at that!"

The tone was furious. Pickings approached.

"Do you see that?" said Booverman, pointing to a freshly laid circle of sod ten inches from his ball. "That, my boy, was where the cup was yesterday. If they hadn't moved the flag two hours ago, I'd have had a three. Now, what do you think of that for rotten luck?"

"Lay it dead," said Pickings, anxiously, shaking his head sympathetically. "The green's a bit fast."

The put ran slowly up to the hole, and stopped four inches short.

"By heavens! why didn't I put over it!" said Booverman, brandishing his putter. "A thirty-foot put that stops an inch short - did you ever see anything like it? By everything that's just and fair I should have had a three. You'd have had it, Picky. Lord! if I only could put!"

"One under three," said Pickings to his fluttering inner self. "He can't realize it. If I can only keep his mind off the score!"

The seventh tee is reached by a carefully planned, fatiguing flight of steps to the top of a bluff, where three churches at the back beckon so many recording angels to swell the purgatory lists. As you advance to the abrupt edge, everything is spread before you; nothing is concealed. In the first plane, the entangling branches of a score of apple-trees are ready to trap a topped ball and bury it under impossible piles of dry leaves. Beyond, the wired tennis-courts give forth a musical, tinny note when attacked. In the middle distance a glorious sycamore draws you to the left, and a file of elms beckon the sliced way to a marsh, wilderness of grass and an overgrown gully whence no balls return. In front, one hundred and twenty yards away, is a formidable bunker, running up to which is a tract of long grass, which two or three times a year is barbered by a charitable enterprise. The seventh hole itself lies two hundred and sixty yards away in a hollow guarded by a sunken ditch, a sure three or - a sure six.

Booverman was still too indignant at the trick fate had played him on the last green to yield to any other emotion. He forgot that a dozen good scores had ended abruptly in the swale to the right. He was only irritated. He plumped down his ball, dug his toes in the ground, and sent off another long, satisfactory drive, which added more fuel to his anger.

"Any one else would have had a three on the six," he muttered as he left the tee. "It's too ridiculous."

He had a short approach and an easy put, plucked his ball from the cup, and said in an injured tone:

"Picky, I feel bad about that sixth hole, and the fourth, too. I've lost a stroke on each of them. I'm playing two strokes more than I ought to be. Hang it all! that sixth wasn't right! You told me the green was fast."

"I'm sorry," said Pickings, feeling his fingers grow cold and clammy on the grip.

The eighth hole has many easy opportunities. It is five hundred and twenty yards long, and things may happen at every stroke. You may begin in front of the tee by burying your ball in the waving grass, which is always permitted a sort of poetical license. There are the traps to the seventh hole to be crossed, and to the right the paralleling river can be reached by a short stab or a long, curling slice, which the prevailing wind obligingly assists to a splashing descent.

"And now we have come to the eighth hole," said Booverman, raising his hat in profound salutation. "Whenever I arrive here with a good score I take from eight to eighteen, I lose one to three balls. On the contrary, when I have an average of six, I always get a five and often a four. How this hole has changed my entire life!" He raised his ball and addressed it tenderly: "And now, little ball, we must part, you and I. It seems a shame; you're the nicest little ball I ever have known. You've stuck to me an awful long while.

It's a shame."

He teed up, and drove his best drive, and followed it with a brassy that laid him twenty yards off the green, where a good approach brought the desired four.

"Even threes," said Pickings to himself, as though he had seen a ghost. Now he was only a golfer of one generation; there was nothing in his inheritance to steady him in such a crisis. He began slowly to disintegrate morally, to revert to type. He contained himself until Booverman had driven free of the river, which flanks the entire green passage to the ninth hole, and then barely controlling the impulse to catch Booverman by the knees and implore him to discretion, he burst out:

"I say, dear boy, do you know what your score is?"

"Something well under four," said Booverman, scratching his head.

"Under four, nothing; even threes!"

"What?"

"Even threes."

They stopped, and tabulated the holes.

"So it is," said Booverman, amazed. "What an infernal pity!"

"Pity?"

"Yes, pity. If only some one else could play it out!"

He studied the hundred and fifty yards that were needed to reach the green that was set in the crescent of surrounding trees, changed his brassy for his cleek, and his cleek for his midiron.

"I wish you hadn't told me," he said nervously.

Pickings on the instant comprehended his blunder. For the first time Booverman's shot went wide of the mark, straight into the trees that bordered the river to the left.

"I'm sorry," said Pickings with a feeble groan.

"My dear Picky, it had to come," said Booverman, with a shrug of his shoulders. "The ball is now lost, and all the score goes into the air, the most miraculous score any one ever heard of is nothing but a crushed egg!"

"It may have bounded back on the course," said Pickings, desperately.

"No, no, Picky; not that. In all the sixty thousand times I have hit trees, barns, car-tracks, caddies, fences, - "

"There it is!" cried Pickings, with a shout of joy.

Fair on the course, at the edge of the green itself, lay the ball, which soon was sunk for a four. Pickings felt a strange, unaccountable desire to leap upon Booverman like a fluffy, enthusiastic dog; but he fought it back with the new sense of responsibility that came to him. So he said artfully: "By George! old man, if you hadn't missed on the fourth or the sixth, you'd have done even threes!"

Owen Johnson

"You know what I ought to do now - I ought to stop," said Booverman, in profound despair - "quit golf and never lift another club. It's a crime to go on; it's a crime to spoil such a record. Twenty-eight for nine holes, only forty-two needed for the next nine to break the record, and I have done it in thirty-three - and in fifty-three! I ought not to try; it's wrong."

He teed his ball for the two-hundred-yard flight to the easy tenth, and took his cleek.

"I know just what'll happen now; I know it well."

But this time there was no varying in the flight; the drive went true to the green, straight on the flag, where a good but not difficult put brought a two.

"Even threes again," said Pickings, but to himself. "It can't go on. It must turn."

"Now, Pickings, this is going to stop," said Booverman angrily. "I'm not going to make a fool of myself. I'm going right up to the tee, and I'm going to drive my ball right smack into the woods and end it. And I don't care."

"What!"

"No, I don't care. Here goes."

Again his drive continued true, the mashy pitch for the second was accurate, and his put, after circling the rim of the cup, went down for a three.

The twelfth hole is another dip into the long grass that might serve as an elephant's bed, and then across the

Housatonic River, a carry of one hundred and twenty yards to the green at the foot of an intruding tree.

"Oh, I suppose I'll make another three here, too," said Booverman, moodily. "That'll only make it worse."

He drove with his midiron high in the air and full on the flag.

"I'll play my put carefully for three," he said, nodding his head. Instead, it ran straight and down for two.

He walked silently to the dreaded thirteenth tee, which, with the returning fourteenth, forms the malignant Scylla and Charybdis of the course. There is nothing to describe the thirteenth hole. It is not really a golf-hole; it is a long, narrow breathing spot, squeezed by the railroad tracks on one side and by the river on the other. Resolute and fearless golfers often cut them out entirely, nor are ashamed to acknowledge their terror. As you stand at the thirteenth tee, everything is blurred to the eye. Near by are rushes and water, woods to the left and right; the river and the railroad; and the dry land a hundred yards away looks tiny and distant, like a rock amid floods.

A long drive that varies a degree is doomed to go out of bounds or to take the penalty of the river.

"Don't risk it. Take an iron - play it carefully," said Pickings in a voice that sounded to his own ears unrecognizable.

Booverman followed his advice and landed by the fence to the left, almost off the fair. A midiron for his second put him in position for another four, and again brought his score to even threes.

When the daring golfer has passed quaking up the narrow way and still survives, he immediately falls a victim to the fourteenth, which is a bend hole, with all the agonies of the preceding thirteenth, augmented by a second shot over a long, mushy pond. If you play a careful iron to keep from the railroad, now on the right, or to dodge the river on your left, you are forced to approach the edge of the swamp with a cautious fifty-yard-running-up stroke before facing the terrors of the carry. A drive with a wooden club is almost sure to carry into the swamp, and only a careful cleek shot is safe.

"I wish I were playing this for the first time," said Booverman, blackly. "I wish I could forget - rid myself of memories. I have seen class A amateurs take twelve, and professionals eight. This is the end of all things, Picky, the saddest spot on earth. I won't waste time. Here goes."

To Pickings's horror, the drive began slowly to slice out of bounds, toward the railroad tracks.

"I knew it," said Booverman, calmly, "and the next will go there, too; then I'll put one in the river, two the swamp, slice into - "

All at once he stopped, thunderstruck. The ball, hitting tire or rail, bounded high in the air, forward, back upon the course, lying in perfect position; Pickings said something in a purely reverent spirit.

"Twice in sixty thousand times," said Booverman, unrelenting. "That only evens up the sixth hole. Twice in sixty thousand times!"

From where the ball lay an easy brassy brought it near enough to the green to negotiate another four. Pickings, trembling like a toy dog in zero weather, reached the green in ten strokes, and took three more puts.

The fifteenth, a short pitch over the river, eighty yards to a slanting green entirely surrounded by more long grass, which gave it the appearance of a chin spot on a full face of whiskers, was Booverman's favorite hole. While Pickings held his eyes to the ground and tried to breathe in regular breaths, Booverman placed his ball, drove with the requisite back spin, and landed dead to the hole. Another two resulted.

"Even threes - fifteen holes in even threes," said Pickings to himself, his head beginning to throb. He wanted to sit down and take his temples in his hands, but for the sake of history he struggled on.

"Damn it!" said Booverman all at once.

"What's the matter?" said Pickings, observing his face black with fury.

"Do you realize, Pickings, what it means to me to have lost those two strokes on the fourth and sixth greens, and through no fault of mine, neither? Even threes for the whole course - that's what I could do if I had those two strokes - the greatest thing that's ever been seen on a golf-course. It may be a hundred years before any human being on the face of this earth will get such a chance. And to think I might have done it with a little luck!"

Pickings felt his heart begin to pump, but he was able to say with some degree of calm:

"You may get a three here."

"Never. Four, three and four is what I'll end."

"Well, good heavens! what do you want?"

"There's no joy in it, though," said Booverman, gloomily. "If I had those two strokes back, I'd go down in history, I'd be immortal. And you, too, Picky, you'd be immortal, because you went around with me. The fourth hole was bad enough, but the sixth was heartbreaking."

His drive cleared another swamp and rolled well down the farther plateau. A long cleek laid his ball off the green, a good approach stopped a little short of the hole, and the put went down.

"Well, that ends it," said Booverman, gloomily.

"I've got to make a two and a three to do it. The two is quite possible; the three absurd."

The seventeenth hole returns to the swamp that enlivens the sixth. It is a full cleek, with about six mental hazards distributed in Indian ambush, and in five of them a ball may lie until the day of judgment before rising again.

Pickings turned his back, unable to endure the agony of watching. The click of the club was sharp and true. He turned to see the ball in full flight arrive unerringly hole high on the green.

"A chance for a two," he said under his breath. He sent two balls into the lost land to the left and one into the rough to the right.

"Never mind me," he said, slashing away in reckless fashion.

Booverman with a little care studied the ten-foot route to the hole and putted down.

"Even threes!" said Pickings, leaning against a tree.

"Blast that sixth hole!" said Booverman, exploding. "Think of what it might be, Picky - what it ought to be!"

Pickings retired hurriedly before the shaking approach of Booverman's frantic club. Incapable of speech, he waved him feebly to drive. He began incredulously to count up again, as though doubting his senses.

"One under three, even threes, one over, even, one under - "

"Here! What the deuce are you doing?" said Booverman, angrily. "Trying to throw me off?"

"I didn't say anything," said Pickings.

"You didn't - muttering to yourself."

"I must make him angry to keep his mind off the score," said Pickings, feebly to himself. He added aloud, "Stop kicking about your old sixth hole! You've had the darndest luck I ever saw, and yet you grumble."

Booverman swore under his breath, hastily approached his ball, drove perfectly, and turned in a rage.

"Luck?" he cried furiously. "Pickings, I've a mind to wring your neck. Every shot I've played has been dead on the pin, now, hasn't it?"

"How about the ninth hole - hitting a tree?"

"Whose fault was that? You had no right to tell me my score, and, besides, I only got an ordinary four there, anyway."

"How about the railroad track?"

"One shot out of bounds. Yes, I'll admit that. That evens up for the fourth."

"How about your first hole in two?"

"Perfectly played; no fluke about it at all - once in sixty thousand times. Well, any more sneers? Anything else to criticize?"

"Let it go at that."

Booverman, in this heckled mood, turned irritably to his ball, played a long midiron, just cleared the crescent bank of the last swale, and ran up on the green.

"Damn that sixth hole!" said Booverman, flinging down his club and glaring at Pickings. "One stroke back, and I could have done it."

Pickings tried to address, but the moment he swung his

club, his legs began to tremble. He shook his head, took a long breath, and picked up his ball.

They approached the green on a drunken run in the wild hope that a short put was possible. Unfortunately the ball lay thirty feet away, and the path to the hole was bumpy and riddled with worm-casts. Still, there was a chance, desperate as it was.

Pickings let his bag slip to the ground and sat down, covering his eyes while Booverman with his putter tried to brush away the ridges.

"Stand up!"

Pickings rose convulsively.

"For heaven's sake, Picky, stand up! Try to be a man!" said Booverman, hoarsely. "Do you think I've any nerve when I see you with chills and fever? Brace up!"

"All right."

Booverman sighted the hole, and then took his stance; but the cleek in his hand shook like an aspen. He straightened up and walked away.

"Picky," he said, mopping his face, "I can't do it. I can't put it."

"You must."

"I've got buck fever. I'll never be able to put it - never."

At the last, no longer calmed by an invincible pessimism, Booverman had gone to pieces. He stood shaking from head to foot.

"Look at that," he said, extending a fluttering hand. "I can't do it; I can never do it."

"Old fellow, you must," said Pickings; "you've got to. Bring yourself together. Here!" He slapped him on the back, pinched his arms, and chafed his fingers. Then he led him back to the ball, braced him into position, and put the putter in his hands.

"Buck fever," said Booverman in a whisper. "Can't see a thing."

Pickings, holding the flag in the cup, said savagely:

"Shoot!"

The ball advanced in a zigzag path, running from worm-cast to a worm-cast, wobbling and rocking, and at the last, as though preordained, fell plump into the cup!

At the same moment, Pickings and Booverman, as though carried off by the same cannon-ball, flattened on the green.

III

Five minutes later, wild-eyed and hilarious, they descended on the clubhouse with the miraculous news. For an hour the assembled golfers roared with laughter as the two stormed, expostulated, and swore to the truth of the tale.

They journeyed from house to house in a vain attempt to find some convert to their claim. For a day they passed as consummate comedians, and the more they yielded to their rage, the more consummate was their art declared. Then a change took place. From laughing the educated town of Stockbridge turned to resentment, then to irritation, and finally to suspicion. Booverman and Pickings began to lose caste, to be regarded as unbalanced, if not positively dangerous. Unknown to them, a committee carefully examined the books of the club. At the next election another treasurer and another secretary were elected.

Since then, month in and month out, day after day, in patient hope, the two discredited members of the educated community of Stockbridge may be seen, *accompanied by caddies*, toiling around the links in a desperate belief that the miracle that would restore them to standing may be repeated. Each time as they arrive nervously at the first tee and prepare to swing, something between a chuckle and a grin runs through the assemblage, while the left eyes contract waggishly, and a murmuring may be heard,

Owen Johnson

"Even threes."

*   *   *   *   *

The Stockbridge golf-links is a course of ravishing beauty and the Housatonic River, as has been said, goes wriggling around it as though convulsed with merriment.

A MAN OF NO IMAGINATION

I

Inspector Frawley, of the Canadian Secret Service, stood at attention, waiting until the scratch of a pen should cease throughout the dim, spacious office and the Honorable Secretary of Justice should acquaint him with his desires.

He held himself deferentially, body compact, eyes clear and steady, face blank and controlled, without distinction, without significance, a man mediocre as a crowd. His hands were joined loosely behind his back; his glance, without deviating, remained persistently on the profile of the Honorable Secretary, as though in that historic room the human note alone could compel his curiosity.

The thin squeak of the pen faded into the silences of the great room. The Secretary of Justice ran his fingers over his forehead, looked up, and met the Inspector's gaze - fixed, profound, and mathematical. With a sudden unease he pushed back his chair, troubled by the analysis of his banal man, who, in another turn of Fate, might pursue him as dispassionately as he now stood before him for his commands. With a few rapid strides he crossed the room, lit a cigar, blew into the swirl of smoke this caprice of his imagination, and returned stolidly, as became a man of facts and figures.

Owen Johnson

Flinging himself loosely in an easy chair, he threw a rapid glance at his watch, locked his fingers, and began with the nervous directness of one who wishes to be rid of formalities:

"Well, Inspector, you returned this morning?"

"An hour ago, sir."

"A creditable bit of work, Inspector Frawley - the department is pleased."

"Thank you indeed, sir."

"Does the case need you any more?"

"I should say not, sir - no, sir."

"You are ready to report for duty?"

"Oh, yes, sir."

"How soon?"

"I think I'm ready now, sir - yes, sir."

"Glad to hear it, Inspector, very glad. You're the one man I wanted." As though the civilities had been sufficiently observed, the Secretary stiffened in his chair and continued rapidly: "It's that Toronto affair; you've read the details. The government lost $350,000. We caught four of the gang, but the ringleader got away with the money. Have you studied it? What did you make of it? Sit down."

Frawley took a chair stiffly, hanging his hat between his knees and considering.

"It did look like work from the States," he said thoughtfully. "I beg pardon, did you say they'd caught some of the gang?"

"Four - this morning. The telegram's just in."

The Honorable Secretary, a little strange yet to the routine of the office, looked at Frawley with a sudden desire to test his memory.

"Do you know the work?" he asked; "could you recognize the ringleader?"

"That might not be so hard, sir," said Frawley, with a nod; "we know pretty well, of course, who's able to handle such jobs as that. Would you have a description anywhere?"

The Honorable Secretary rose, took from his desk a paper, and began to read. In his seat Inspector Frawley crossed his legs carefully, drew his fists up under his chin, and stared at the reader, but without focusing his glance on him. Once during the recital he started at some item of description, but immediately relaxed. The report finished, the Secretary let it drop into his lap and waited, impressed, despite himself, at the thought of the immense galleries of crime through which the Inspector was seeking his victim. All at once into the unseeing stare there flickered a light of understanding. Frawley returned to the room, saw the Secretary, and nodded.

"It's Bucky," he said tentatively. A moment his glance

went reflectively to a far corner, then he nodded slowly, looked at the Secretary, and said with conviction: "It looks very much, sir, like Bucky Greenfield."

"It is Greenfield," replied the Secretary, without attempting to conceal his astonishment.

"I would like to observe," said Frawley thoughtfully, without noticing his surprise, "that there is a bit of an error in that description, sir. It's the left ear that's broken. Furthermore, he don't toe out - excepting when he does it on a purpose. So it's Bucky Greenfield I'm to bring back, sir?"

The Secretary nodded, penciling Frawley's correction on the paper.

"Bucky - well, now, that is odd!" said Frawley musingly. He rose and took a step to the desk. "Very odd." Mechanically he saw the straggling papers on the top and arranged them into orderly piles. "Well, he can't say I didn't warn him!"

"What!" broke in the Secretary in quick astonishment, "you know the fellow?"

"Indeed, yes, sir," said Frawley, with a nod. "We know most of the crooks in the States. We're good friends, too - so long as they stay over the line. It's useful, you know. So I'm to go after Bucky?"

The Secretary, judging the moment had arrived to be impressive, said solemnly:

"Inspector Frawley, if you have to stick to it until he dies of old age, you're never to let up until you get

Bucky Greenfield! While the British Empire holds together, no man shall rob Her Majesty of a farthing and sleep in security. You understand the situation?"

"I do, sir."

The Honorable Secretary, only half satisfied, continued:

"Your credit is unlimited - there'll be no question of that. If you need to buy up a whole South American government - buy it! By the way, he will make for South America, will he not?"

"Probably - yes, sir. Chile or the Argentine - there's no extradition treaty there."

"But even then," broke in the Secretary with a nervous frown - "there are ways - other ways?"

"Oh, yes." Frawley, picking up a paper-cutter, stood by the mantel tapping his palm. "Oh, yes - there are other ways! So it's Bucky - well, I warned him!"

"Now, Inspector, to settle the matter," interrupted the Secretary, anxious to return to his routine, "when can you go on the case?"

"If the papers are ready, sir - "

"They are - everything. The Home Office has been cabled. To-morrow every British official throughout the world will be notified to render you assistance and honor your drafts."

Inspector Frawley heard with approval and consulted

his watch.

"There's an express for New York leaves at noon," he said reflectively - then, with a glance at the clock, "thirty-five minutes; I can make that, sir."

"Good, very good."

"If I might suggest, sir - if the Inspector who has had the case in hand could go a short distance with me?"

"Inspector Keech shall join you at the station."

"Thank you, sir. Is there anything further?"

The Secretary shook his head, and springing up, held out his hand enthusiastically.

"Good luck to you, Inspector - you have a big thing ahead of you, a very big thing."

"Thank you, sir."

"By the way - you're not married?"

"No, sir."

"This is pretty short notice. How long have you been on this other case?"

"A trifle over six months, sir."

"Don't you want a couple of days to rest up? I can let you have that very easily."

" It really makes no difference - I think I'll leave

to-day, sir."

"Oh, a moment more, Inspector - "

Frawley halted.

"How long do you think this ought to take you?"

Frawley considered, and answered carefully:

"It'll be long, I think. You see, there are several circumstances that are unusual about this case."

"How so?"

"Well, Buck is clever - there's no gainsaying that - quite at the top of the profession. Then, he's expecting me."

"You?"

"They're a queer lot," Frawley explained with a touch of pride. "Crooks are full of little vanities. You see, Bucky knows I've never dropped a trail, and I think it's rather gotten on his nerves. I think he wasn't satisfied until he dared me. He's very odd - very odd indeed. It's a little personal. I doubt, sir, if I bring him back alive."

"Inspector Frawley," said the new Secretary, "I hope I have sufficiently impressed upon you the importance of your mission."

Frawley stared at his chief in surprise.

"I'm to stick to him until I get him," he said in wonder; "that's all, isn't it, sir?"

Owen Johnson

The Secretary, annoyed by his lack of imagination, essayed a final phrase.

"Inspector, this is my last word," he said with a frown; "remember that you represent Her Majesty's government - you are Her Majesty's government! I have confidence in you."

"Thank you, sir."

Frawley moved slowly to the door and with his hand on the knob hesitated. The Secretary saw in the movement a reluctance to take the decisive step that must open before him the wide stretches of the world.

"After all, he must have a speck of imagination," he thought, reassured.

"I beg pardon, sir."

Frawley had turned in embarrassment.

"Well, Inspector, what can I do for you?"

"If you please, sir," said Frawley, "I was just thinking - after all, it has been a bit of a while since I've been home - indeed, I should like it very much if I could take a good English mutton-chop and a musty ale at old Nell's, sir. I can still get the two o'clock express."

"Granted!"

"If you'd prefer not, sir," said Frawley, surprised at the vexation in his answer.

" Not at all - take the two o'clock - good day ,

good day!"

Inspector Frawley, sorely puzzled, shifted his balance, opened his mouth, then with a bob of his head answered hastily:

"A - good day, sir!"

II

Sam Greenfield, known as "Bucky," age about 42, height about 5 feet 10 inches, weight between 145 and 150. Hair mouse-colored, thinning out over forehead, parted in middle, showing scalp beneath; mustache would be lighter than hair - if not dyed; usually clipped to about an inch. Waxy complexion, light blue eyes a little close together, thin nose, a prominent dimple on left cheek - may wear whiskers. Laughs in low key. Left ear lobe broken. Slightly bowlegged. While in conversation strokes chin. When standing at a counter or bar goes through motions, as if jerking himself together, crowding his elbows slowly to his side for a moment, then, throwing back his head, jumps up from his heels. When dreaming, attempts to bite mustache with lower lip. When he sits in a chair places himself sidewise and hangs both arms over back. In walking strikes back part of heel first, and is apt to waver from time to time. Dresses neatly, carries hands in side-pockets only - plays piano constantly, composing as he goes along. During day smokes twenty to thirty cigarettes, cutting them in half for cigarette-holder and throwing them away after three or four whiffs. After dinner invariably smokes one cigar. Cut is good likeness. Cut of signature is facsimile of his original writing.

With this overwhelming indictment against the liberty

of the fugitive, to escape which Greenfield would have to change his temperament as well as his physical aspect, Inspector Frawley took the first steamer from New York to the Isthmus of Panama.

He had slight doubt of Greenfield's final destination, for the flight of the criminal is a blind instinct for the south as though a frantic return to barbarism. At this time Chile and the Argentine had not yet accepted the principle of extradition, and remained the Mecca of the lawbreakers of the world.

Yet though Frawley felt certain of Greenfield's objective, he did not at once strike for the Argentine. The Honorable Secretary of Justice had eliminated the necessity for considering time. Frawley had no need to guess, nor to risk. He had simply to become a wheel in the machinery of the law, to grind slowly, tirelessly, and inexorably. This idea suited admirably his temperament and his desires.

He arrived at Colon, took train for Panama across the laborious path where a thousand little men were scratching endlessly, and on the brink of the Pacific began his search. No one had heard of Greenfield.

At the end of a week's waiting he boarded a steamer and crawled down the western coast of South America, investigating every port, braving the yellow fever at Guayaquil, Ecuador, and facing a riot at Callao, Peru, before he found at Lima the trail of the fugitive. Greenfield had passed the day there and left for Chile. Dragging each intermediate port with the same caution, Frawley followed the trail to Valparaiso. Greenfield had stayed a week and again departed.

Owen Johnson

Frawley at once took steamer for the Argentine, passed down the tongue of South America, through the Straits of Magellan, and arrived at length in the harbor of Buenos Ayres.

An hour later, as he took his place at the table in the Criterion Gardens, a hand fell on his shoulder and some one at his back said:

"Well, Bub!"

He turned. A thin man of medium height, with blue eyes and yellow complexion, was laughing in expectation of his discomfiture. Frawley laid down the menu carefully, raised his head, and answered quietly:

"Why, how d'ye do, Bucky?"

III

"We shake, of course," said Greenfield, holding out his hand.

"Why not? Sit down."

The fugitive slid into a chair and hung his arms over the back, asking immediately:

"What took you so long? You're after me, of course?"

"Am I?" Frawley answered, looking at him steadily. Greenfield, with a twitch of his shoulders, returned to his question:

"What took you so long? Didn't you guess I'd come direct?"

"I'm not guessing," said Frawley.

"What do you say to dining on me?" said Greenfield with a malicious smile. "I owe you that. I clipped your vacation pretty short. Besides - guess you know it yourself - you can't touch me here. Why not talk things over frankly? Say, Bub, shall it be on me?"

"I'm willing."

A waiter sidled up and took the order that Greenfield gave without hesitation.

"You see, even the dinner was ready for you," he said with a wink; "see how you like it." With a gesture of impatience he pushed aside the menu, squared his arms on the table, and looked suddenly at his pursuer with the deviltry of a schoolboy glistening in his eyes. "Well, Bub, I went into your all-fired Canady!"

"So you did - why?"

"Well," said Greenfield, drawing lines with his knife-point on the nap, "one reason was I wanted to see if Her Majesty's shop has such an all-fired long arm - "

"And the other reason was I warned you to keep over the line."

"Why, Bub, you *are* a bright boy!"

"It ain't me, Bucky," Frawley answered, with a shake of his head; "it's the all-fired government that's after you."

"Good - first rate - then we'll have a little excitement!"

"You'll have plenty of that, Bucky!"

"Maybe, Bub, maybe. Well, I made a neat job of it, didn't I?"

"You did," admitted Frawley with an appreciative nod. "But you were wrong - you were wrong - you should have kept off. The Canadian Government ain't like your bloomin' democracy. It don't forgive - it don't forget. Tack that up, Bucky. It's a principle we've got at stake with you!"

"Don't I know it?" cried Greenfield, striking the table. "What else do you think I did it for?"

Frawley gazed at him, then said slowly: "I told them it was a personal matter."

"Sure it was! Do you think I could keep out after you served notice on me? D - your English pride and your English justice! I'm a good enough Yank to see if your dinky police is such an all-fired cute little bunch of wonder-workers as you say! Bub - you think you're going to get Mr. Greenfield - don't you?"

"I'm not thinking, Bucky - "

"Eh?"

"I'm simply sticking to you."

"Sticking to me!" cried Greenfield with a roar of disgust. "Why, you unimaginative, lumbering, beef-eating Canuck, you can't get me that way! Why in tarnation didn't you strike plump for here - instead of rubbin' yourself down the whole coast of South Ameriky?"

"Bucky, you don't understand the situation properly," objected Frawley, without varying the level tone of his voice. "Supposing it had been a bloomin' corporation had sent me - ? that's what I'd have done. But it's the government this time - Her Majesty's government! Time ain't no consideration. I'd have raked down the whole continent if I'd had to - though I knew where you were."

"Well, and now what? You can't touch me, Bub," he added earnestly. "I like straight talk, man to man. Now, what's your game?"

"Business."

"All right then," said Greenfield, with a frown, "but you can't touch me - now. There's an extradition treaty coming, but then there'd have to be a retroactive clause to do you any good." He paused, studying the expression on the Inspector's face. "There's enough of the likes of me here to see that don't occur. Say, Bub?"

"Well?"

"You deal a square pack, don't you?"

"That's my reputation, Bucky."

"Give me your word you'll play me square."

Inspector Frawley, leaning forward, helped himself busily. Greenfield, with pursed lips, studied every movement.

"No kidnapping tricks?"

Without lifting his eyes Frawley sharpened his knife vigorously against his fork and fell to eating.

"Well, Bub?"

"What?"

"No fancy kidnapping?"

"I'm promising nothing, Bucky."

There was a blank moment while Greenfield considered. Suddenly he shot out his hand, saying with a nod: "You're a white man, Bub, and I never heard a word against that." He filled a glass and shoved it toward Frawley. "We might as well clink on it. For I rather opinionate before we get through this little business - there'll be something worth talking about."

"Here's to you then, Bucky," said Frawley, nodding.

"Remember what I tell you," said Greenfield, looking over his glass, "there's going to be something to live for."

"I say, Bucky," said Frawley with a lazy interest, "would they serve you five-o'clock tea here, I wonder?"

Greenfield, drawing back, laughed a superior laugh.

"Bub, I'm sorry for you - 'pon my word I am."

"How so, Bucky?"

"Why, you plodding little English lamb, you don't have the slightest suspicion what you're gettin' into!"

"What am I getting into, Bucky?"

Greenfield threw back his head with a chuckle.

"If you get me, it'll be the last job you ever pull off."

"Maybe, maybe."

"Since things are aboveboard - listen here," said Greenfield with sudden seriousness. "Bub, you'll not get me alive. Nothing personal, you understand, but it'll have to be your life or mine. If it comes to the pinch, look out for yourself - "

"Oh, yes," said Frawley, with a matter-of-fact nod, "I understand."

"I ain't tried to bribe you," said Greenfield, rising. "Thank me for that - though another man might have been sent up for life."

"Thanks," Frawley said with a drawl. "And you'll notice I haven't advised you to come back and face the music. Seems to me we understand each other."

"Here's my address," said Greenfield, handing him a card; "may save you some trouble. I'm here every night." He held out his hand. "Turn up and meet the profesh. They're a clever lot here. They'd appreciate meeting you, too."

"Perhaps I will."

"Ta-ta, then."

Greenfield took a few steps, halted, and lounged back with a smile full of mischief.

"By the way, Bub - how long has Her Majesty's dinkies given you?"

"It's a life appointment, Bucky."

"Really - bless me - then your bloomin' government has some sense after all."

The two men saluted gravely, with a parting exchange.

"Now, Bub - keep fit."

"Same to you, Bucky."

Owen Johnson

IV

The view of Greenfield sauntering lightly away among the noisy tables, bravado in his manner, deviltry in his heart, was the last glimpse Inspector Frawley was destined to have of him in many months. True, Greenfield had not lied: the address was genuine, but the man was gone. For days Frawley had the city scoured without gaining a clue. No steamer had left the harbor, not even a tramp. If Greenfield was not in hiding, he must have buried himself in the interior.

It was a week before Frawley found the track. Greenfield had walked thirty miles into the country and taken the train for Rio Mendoza on the route across the Andes to Valparaiso.

Frawley followed the same day, somewhat mystified at this sudden change of base. In the train the thermometer stood at 116 deg.. The heat made of everything a solitude. Frawley, lifeless, stifling, and numbed, glued himself to the air-holes with eyes fastened on the horizon, while the train sped across the naked, singeing back of the plains like the welt that springs to meet the fall of the lash. For two nights he watched the distended sun, exhausted by its own madness, drop back into the heated void, and the tortured stars rise over the stricken desert. At the end of thirty-six hours of agony he arrived at Rio Mendoza. Thence he reached Punta de Vacas, procured mules and a guide, and prepared for the ascent over the mountains.

At two o'clock the next morning he began to climb out of hell. The tortured plains settled below him. A divine freshness breathed upon him with a new hope of life. He left the burning conflict of summer and passed into the aroma of spring.

Then the air grew intense, a new suffocation pressed about his temples - the suffocation of too much life. In an hour he had run the gamut of the seasons. The cold of everlasting winter descended and stung his senses. Up and up and up they went - then suddenly down, with the half-breed guide and the tireless mule always at the same distance before him; and again began the insistent mechanical toiling upward. He grew listless and indifferent, acquiescent in these steep efforts that the next moment must throw away. The horror of immense distance rose about him. From time to time a stone dislodged by their passage rushed from under him, struck the brink, and spun into the void, to fall endlessly. The face of the earth grew confused and dropped in a mist from before his eyes.

Then as they toiled still upward, a gale as though sent in anger rushed down upon them, sweeping up whirlwinds of snow, raging and shrieking, dragging them to the brink, and threatening to blot them out.

Frawley clutched the saddle, then flung his arms about the neck of his mule. His head was reeling, the indignant blood rushed to his nostrils and his ears, his lungs no longer could master the divine air. Then suddenly the mules stopped, exhausted. Through the maelstrom the guide shrieked to him not to use the spur. Frawley felt himself in danger of dying, and had no resentment.

For a day they affronted the immense wilds until they had forced themselves thousands of feet above the race of men. Then they began to descend.

Below them the clouds lapped and rolled like the elements before the creation. Still they descended, and the moist oblivion closed about them, like the curse of a world without color. The bleak mists separated and began to roll up above them, a cloud split asunder, and through the slit the earth jumped up, and the solid land spread before them as when at the dawn it obeyed the will of the Creator. They saw the hills and the mountains grow, and the rivers trickle toward the sea. The masses of brown and green began to be splashed with red and yellow as the fields became fertile and fructified; and the insect race of men began to crawl to and fro.

The half-breed, who saw the scene for the hundredth time, bent his head in awe. Frawley straightened in his saddle, stretched the stiffness out of his limbs, patted his mule solicitously, glanced at the guide, and stopped in perplexity at the mute, reverential attitude.

"What's he starin' at now?" he muttered in as then, with a glance at his watch, he added anxiously, "I say, Sammy, when do we get a bit to eat?"

V

In Valparaiso he readily found the track of Greenfield. Up to the time of his departure, two boats had sailed: one for the north, and one by the Straits of Magellan to Buenos Ayres. Greenfield had bought a ticket for each, after effecting the withdrawal of his account at a local bank. Frawley was in perplexity: for Greenfield to flee north was to run into the jaws of the law. The withdrawal of the account decided him. He returned to Buenos Ayres by the route he had come, arriving the day before the steamer. To his discomfiture Greenfield was not on board. By ridiculously casting away his protection he had thrown the detective off the track and gained three weeks. Without more concern than he might have shown in taking a trip from Toronto to New York, Frawley a third time crossed the Andes and set himself to correcting his first error.

He traced Greenfield laboriously up the coast back to Panama and there lost the trail. At the end of two months he learned that Greenfield had shipped as a common sailor on a freighter that touched at Hawaii. From here he followed him to Yokohama, Singapore, Ceylon, and Bombay.

Thence Greenfield, suddenly abandoning the water route, had proceeded by land to Bagdad, and across the Turkish Empire to Constantinople. Without a pause,

Frawley traced him next into the Balkans, through Bulgaria, Roumania, amid massacre and revolution to Budapest, back to Odessa, and across the back of Russia by Moscow and Riga to Stockholm. A year had elapsed.

Several times he might have gained on the fugitive had he trusted to his instinct; but he bided his time, renouncing a stroke of genius, in order to be certain of committing no error, awaiting the moment when Greenfield would pause and he might overtake him. But the fugitive, as though stung by a gad-fly, continued to plunge madly over sea and continent. Four months, five months behind, Frawley continued the tireless pursuit.

From Stockholm the chase led to Copenhagen, to Christiansand, down the North Sea to Rotterdam. From thence Greenfield had rushed by rail to Lisbon and taken steamer to Africa, touching at Gibraltar, Portuguese and French Guinea, Sierra Leone, and proceeding thence into the Congo. For a month all traces disappeared in the veldt, until by chance, rather than by his own merits, Frawley found the trail anew in Madagascar, whither Greenfield had come after a desperate attempt to bury his trail on the immense plains of Southern Africa.

From Madagascar, Frawley followed him to Aden in Arabia and by steamer to Melbourne. Again for weeks he sought the confused track vainly through Australia, up through Sydney, down again to Tasmania and New Zealand on a false clue, back to Queensland, where at last in Cooktown he learned anew of the passing of his man.

The third year began without appreciable gain. Greenfield still was three months in advance, never pausing, scurrying from continent to continent, as though instinctively aware of the progress of his pursuer.

In this year Frawley visited Sumatra, Java, and Borneo, stopped at Manila, jumped immediately to Korea, and hurried on to Vladivostok, where he found that Greenfield had procured passage on a sealer bound for Auckland. There he had taken the steamer by the Straits of Magellan back to Buenos Ayres.

There, within the first hour, he heard a report that his man had gone on to Rio Janeiro, caught the cholera, and died there. Undaunted by the epidemic, Frawley took the next boat and entered the stricken city by swimming ashore. For a week he searched the hospitals and the cemeteries. Greenfield had indeed been stricken, but, escaping with his life, had left for the northern part of Brazil. The delay resulted in a gain of three months for Frawley, but without heat or excitement he began anew the pursuit, passing up the coast to Para and the mouth of the Amazon, by Bogota and Panama into Mexico, on up toward the border of Texas. The months between him and Greenfield shortened to weeks, then to days without troubling his equanimity. At El Paso he arrived a few hours after Greenfield had left, going toward the Salt Basin and the Guadalupe Mountains. Frawley took horses and a guide and followed to the edge of the desert. At three o'clock in the afternoon a horseman grew out of the horizon, a figure that remained stationary and attentive, studying his approach through a spy-glass. Suddenly, as though satisfied, the stranger took off his hat and waved it above his head in challenge, and digging his heels into his horse, disappeared into the desert.

VI

Frawley understood the challenge - the end was to be in the desert. Failing to move his guide by threat or promise, he left him clamoring frantically on the edge of the desert and rode on toward where the figure of Greenfield had disappeared on the horizon in a puff of dust.

For three days they went their way grimly into the parched sands, husbanding every particle of strength, within plain sight of each other, always at the same unvarying walk. At night they slept by fits and starts, with an ear trained for the slightest hostile sound. Then they cast aside their saddles, their rifles, and super-fluous clothing, in a vain effort to save their mounts.

The horses, heaving and staggering, crawled over the yielding sands like silhouettes drawn by a thread. In the sky not a cloud appeared; below, the yellow monotony extended as flat as a dish. Above them a lazy buzzard, wheeling in languid circles, followed with patient conviction.

On the fourth morning Frawley's horse stopped, shuddered, and went down in a heap. Greenfield halted and surveyed his discomfiture grimly, without a sign of elation.

"That's bad, very bad," Frawley said judicially. "I ought to have sent word to the department. Still, it's not over yet - his horse won't last long. Well, I mustn't carry much."

He abandoned his revolver, a knife, $200 in gold, and continued on foot, preserving only the water-bag with its precious mouthful. Greenfield, who had waited immovably, allowed him to approach within a quarter of a mile before putting his horse in motion.

"He's going to make sure I stay here," said Frawley to himself, seeing that Greenfield made no attempt to increase the lead. "Well, we'll see."

Twelve hours later Greenfield's horse gave out. Frawley uttered a cry of joy, but the handicap of half a day was a serious one; he was exhausted, famished, and in the bag there remained only sufficient water to moisten his lips.

The fifth day broke with an angry sun and no sign on the horizon to relieve the eternal monotony. Only the buzzard at the same distance aloft bided his time. Hunter and hunted, united perforce by their common suffering, plodded on with the weary, hopeless straining of human beings harnessed to a plow, covering scarcely a mile an hour. From time to time, by common consent, they sat down, gaunt, exhausted figures, eyeing each other with the instinct of beasts, their elbows on their bony knees. Whether from a fear of losing energy, whether under the spell of the frightful stillness, neither had uttered a word.

Frawley was afire with thirst. The desert entered his body with its dry mortal heat, and ran its consuming dryness through his veins; his eyes started from his face as the sun above him hung out of the parched sky. He began to talk to himself, to sing. Under his feet the sand sifted like the soft protest of autumn leaves. He imagined himself back in the forest, marking the rustle of leafy branches and the intermittent dropping of acorns and twigs. All at once his legs refused to move. He stood still, his gaze concentrated on the figure of Greenfield a long moment, then his body crumpled under him and he sank without volition to the ground.

Greenfield stopped, sat down, and waited. After half an hour he drew himself to his feet, moved on, then stopped, returned, approached, and listened to the crooning of the delirious man. Suddenly satisfied, he flung both arms into the air in frenzied triumph, turned, staggered, and reeled away, while back over the desert came the grotesque, hideous refrain, in maddened victory:

"Yankee Doodle Dandy oh!
Yankee Doodle Dandy!"

Frawley watched him go, then with a sigh of relief turned his glance to the black revolving form in the air - at least that remained to break the horror of the solitude. Then he lost consciousness.

The beat of wings across his face aroused him with a start and a cry of agony. The great bird of carrion, startled in its inspection, flew clumsily off and settled fearlessly on the ground, blinking at him.

An immense revolt, a furious anger brought with it new strength. He rose and rushed at the bird with clenched fist, cursing it as it lumbered awkwardly away. Then he began desperately to struggle on, following the tracks in the sand.

At the end of an hour specks appeared on the horizon. He looked at them in his delirium and began to laugh uneasily.

"I must be out of my head," he said to himself seriously. "It's a mirage. Well, I suppose it is the end. Who'll they put on the case now? Keech, I suppose; yes, Keech; he's a good man. Of course it's a mirage."

As he continued to stumble forward, the dots assumed the shape of trees and hills. He laughed contemptuously and began to remonstrate with himself, repeating:

"It's a mirage, or I'm out of my head." He began to be worried, saying over and over: "That's a bad sign, very bad. I mustn't lose control of myself. I must stick to him - stick to him until he dies of old age. Bucky Greenfield! Well, he won't get out of this either. If the department could only know!"

The nearer he drew to life, the more indignant he became. He arrived thus at the edge of trees and green things.

"Why don't they go?" he said angrily. "They ought to, now. Come, I think I'm keeping my head remarkably well."

All at once a magnificent idea came to him - he would walk through the mirage and end it. He advanced furiously against an imaginary tree, struck his forehead, and toppled over insensible.

VII

Frawley returned to consciousness to find himself in the hut of a half-breed Indian, who was forcing a soup of herbs between his lips.

Two days later he regained his strength sufficiently to reach a ranch owned by Englishmen. Fitted out by them, he started at once to return to El Paso; to take up the unending search anew.

In the late afternoon, tired and thirsty, he arrived at a shanty where a handful of Mexican children were lolling in the cool of the wall. At the sound of his approach a woman came running to the door, shrieking for assistance in a Mexican gibberish. He ran hastily to the house, his hand on his pistol. The woman, without stopping her chatter, huddled in the doorway, pointing to the dim corner opposite. Frawley, following her glance, saw the figure of a man stretched on a hasty bed of leaves. He took a few quick steps and recognized Greenfield.

At the same moment the bundle shot to a sitting position, with a cry:

"Who's that?"

Frawley , with a quick motion, covered him with his

revolver, crying:

"Hands up. It's me, Bucky, and I've got you now!"

"Frawley!"

"That's it, Bucky - Hands up!"

Greenfield, without obeying, stared at him wildly.

"God, it is Frawley!" he cried, and fell back in a heap.

Inspector Frawley, advancing a step, repeated his command with no uncertain ring:

"Hands up! Quick!"

On the bed the distorted body contracted suddenly into a ball.

"Easy, Bub," Greenfield said between his teeth. "Easy; don't get excited. I'm dying."

"You?"

Frawley approached cautiously, suspiciously.

"Fact. I'm cashin' in."

"What's the matter?"

"Bug. Plain bug - the desert did the rest."

"A what?"

"Tarantula bite - don't laugh, Bub."

Frawley, at his side, needed but a glance to see that it was true. He ran his hand over Greenfield's belt and removed his pistol.

"Sorry," he said curtly, standing up.

"Quite keerect, Bub!"

"Can I do anything for you?"

"Nope."

Suddenly, without warning, Greenfield raised himself, glared at him, stretched out his hands, and fell into a passionate fit of weeping. Frawley's English reserve was outraged.

"What's the matter?" he said angrily. "You're not going to show the white feather now, are you?"

With an oath Greenfield sat bolt upright, silent and flustered.

"D - you, Bub - show some imagination," he said after a pause. "Do you think I mind dying - me? That's a good one. It ain't that - no - it's ending, ending like this. After all I've been through, to be put out of business by a bug - an ornery little bug."

Then Frawley comprehended his mistake.

"I say, Bucky, I'll take that back," he said awkwardly.

"No imagination, no imagination," Greenfield muttered, sinking back. "Why, man, if I'd chased you three times around the world and got you, I'd fall on you and beat you to a pulp or - or I'd hug you like a long-lost brother."

"I asked your pardon," said Frawley again.

"All right, Bub - all right," Greenfield answered with a short laugh. Then after a pause he added seriously: "So you've come - well, I'm glad it's over. Bub," he continued, raising himself excitedly on his elbow, "here's something strange, only you won't understand it. Do you know, the whole time I knew just where you were - I had a feeling somewhere in the back of my neck. At first you were 'way off, over the horizon; then you got to be a spot coming over the hill. Then I began to feel that spot growin' bigger and bigger - after Rio Janeiro, crawling up, creeping up. Gospel truth, I felt you sneaking up on my back. It got on my nerves. I dreamed about it, and that morning on the trail when you was just a speck on any old hoss - I knew! You - you don't understand such things, Bub, do you?"

Frawley made an effort, failed, and answered helplessly:

"No, Bucky, no, I can't say I do understand."

"Why do you think I ran you into Rio Janeiro?" said Greenfield, twisting on the leaves. "Into the cholery? What do you think made me lay for this desert? Bub, you were on my back, clinging like a catamount. I was bound to shake you off. I was desperate. It had to end one way or t'other. That's why I stuck to you until I thought it was over with you."

"Why didn't you make sure of it?" said Frawley with curiosity; "you could have done for me there."

Greenfield looked at him hard and nodded.

"Keerect, Bub; quite so!"

"Why didn't you?"

"Why!" cried Greenfield angrily. "Ain't you ever had any imagination? Did I want to shoot you down like a common ordinary pickpocket after taking you three times around the world? That was no ending! God, what a chase it was!"

"It was long, Bucky," Frawley admitted. "It was a good one!"

"Can't you understand anything?" Greenfield cried querulously. "Where's anything bigger, more than what we've done? And to have it end like this - to have a bug - a miserable, squashy bug beat you after all!"

For a long moment there was no sound, while Greenfield lay, twisting, his head averted, buried in the leaves.

"It's not right, Bucky," said Frawley at last, with an effort at sympathy. "It oughtn't to have ended this way."

"It was worth it!" Greenfield cried. "Three years! There ain't much dirt we haven't kicked up! Asia, Africa - a regular Cook's tour through Europe, North and South Ameriky. And what seas, Bub!" His voice faltered. The drops of sweat stood thickly on his forehead; but he pulled himself together gamely. "Do you remember the Sea of Japan with its funny little toy junks? Man, we've beaten out Columbus, Jools Verne, and the rest of them - hollow, Bub!"

"I say, what did you do it for?"

"You are a rum un," said Greenfield with a broken laugh. The words began to come shorter and with effort. "Excitement, Bub! Deviltry and cussedness!"

"How do you feel, Bucky?" asked Frawley.

"Half in hell already - stewing for my sins - but it's not that - it's - "

"What, Bucky?"

"That bug! Me, Bucky Greenfield - to go down and out on account of a bug - a little squirmy bug! But I swear even he couldn't have done it if the desert hadn't put me out of business first! No, by God! I'm not downed so easy as that!"

Frawley, in a lame attempt to show his sympathy, went closer to the dying man:

"I say, Bucky."

"Shout away."

"Wouldn't you like to go out, standing, on your feet - with your boots on?"

Greenfield laughed, a contented laugh.

"What's the matter, pal?" said Frawley, pausing in surprise.

"You darned old Englishman," said Greenfield affectionately. "Say, Bub."

"Yes, Bucky."

"The dinkies are all right - but - but a Yank, a real Yank, would 'a' got me in six months."

"All right, Bucky. Shall I raise you up?"

"H'ist away."

"Would you like the feeling of a gun in your hand again?" said Frawley, raising him up.

This time Greenfield did not laugh, but his hand closed convulsively over the butt, and he gave a savage sigh of delight. His limbs contracted violently, his head bore heavily on the shoulder of Frawley, who heard him whisper again:

"A bug - a little - "

Then he stopped and appeared to listen. Outside, the evening was soft and stirring. Through the door the children appeared, tumbling over one another, in grotesque attitudes.

Suddenly, as though in the breeze he had caught the sound of a step, Greenfield jerked almost free of Frawley's arms, shuddered, and fell back rigid. The pistol, flung into the air, twirled, pitched on the floor, and remained quiet.

Frawley placed the body back on the bed of leaves, listened a moment, and rose satisfied. He threw a

Owen Johnson

blanket over the face, picked up the revolver, searched a moment for his hat, and went out to arrange with the Mexican for the night. In a moment he returned and took a seat in the corner, and began carefully to jot down the details on a piece of paper. Presently he paused and looked reflectively at the bed of leaves.

"It's been a good three years," he said reflectively. He considered a moment, rapping the pencil against his teeth, and repeated: "A good three years. I think when I get home I'll ask for a week or so to stretch myself." Then he remembered with anxiety how Greenfield had railed at his lack of imagination and pondered a moment seriously. Suddenly, as though satisfied, he said with a nod of conviction:

"Well, now, we did jog about a bit!"

LARRY MOORE

I

The base-ball season had closed, and we were walking down Fifth avenue, Larry Moore and I. We were discussing the final series for the championship, and my friend was estimating his chances of again pitching the Giants to the top, when a sudden jam on the avenue left us an instant looking face to face at a woman and a child seated in a luxurious victoria.

Larry Moore, who had hold of my arm, dropped it quickly and wavered in his walk. The woman caught her breath and put her muff hastily to her face; but the child saw us without surprise. All had passed within a second, yet I retained a vivid impression of a woman of strange attraction, elegant and indolent, with something in her face which left me desirous of seeing it again, and of a pretty child who seemed a little too serious for that happy age. Larry Moore forgot what he had begun to say. He spoke no further word, and I, in glancing at his face, comprehended that, incredible as it seemed, there was some bond between the woman I had seen and this raw-boned, big-framed, and big-hearted idol of the bleachers.

Without comment I followed Larry Moore, serving his mood as he immediately left the avenue and went east.

At first he went with excited strides, then he slowed down to a profound and musing gait, then he halted, laid his hand heavily on my shoulder, and said:

"Get into the car, Bob. Come up to the rooms."

I understood that he wished to speak to me of what had happened, and I followed. We went thus, without another word exchanged, to his rooms, and entered the little parlor hung with the trophies of his career, which I looked at with some curiosity. On the mantel in the center I saw at once a large photograph of the Hon. Joseph Gilday, a corporation lawyer of whom we reporters told many hard things, a picture I did not expect to find here among the photographs of the sporting celebrities who had sent their regards to my friend of the diamond. In some perplexity I approached and saw across the bottom written in large firm letters: "I'm proud to know you, Larry Moore."

I smiled, for the tribute of the great man of the law seemed incongruous here to me, who knew of old my simple-minded, simple-hearted friend whom, the truth be told, I patronized perforce. Then I looked about more carefully, and saw a dozen photographs of a woman, sometimes alone, sometimes holding a pretty child, and the faces were the faces I had seen in the victoria. I feigned not to have seen them; but Larry, who had watched me, said:

"Look again, Bob; for that is the woman you saw in the carriage, and that is the child."

So I took up a photograph and looked at it long. The face had something more dangerous than beauty in it - the face of a Cleopatra with a look in the deep restless eyes I did not fancy; but I did not tell that to Larry Moore. Then I put it back in its place and turned and said gravely:

"Are you sure that you want to tell me, Larry Moore?"

"I do," he said. "Sit down."

He did not seek preliminaries, as I should have done, but began at once, simply and directly - doubtless he was retelling the story more to himself than to me.

"She was called Fanny Montrose," he said, "a slip of a girl, with wonderful golden hair, and big black eyes that made me tremble, the day I went into the factory at Bridgeport, the day I fell in love. 'I'm Larry Moore; you may have heard of me,' I said, going straight up to her when the whistle blew that night, 'and I'd like to walk home with you, Fanny Montrose.'

"She drew back sort of quick, and I thought she'd been hearing tales of me up in Fall River; so I said: 'I only meant to be polite. You may have heard a lot of bad of me, and a lot of it's true, but you never heard of Larry Moore's being disrespectful to a lady,' and I looked her in the eye and said: 'Will you let me walk home with you, Fanny Montrose?'

"She swung on her foot a moment, and then she said: 'I will.'

"I heard a laugh go up at that, and turned round, with the bit in my teeth; but it was only the women, and you can't touch them. Fanny Montrose hurried on, and I saw she was upset by it, so I said humbly: 'You're not sorry now, are you?'

"'Oh, no,' she said.

"'Will you catch hold of my arm?' I asked her.

"She looked first in my face, and then she slipped in her hand so prettily that it sent all the words from my tongue. 'You've just come to Bridgeport, ain't you?' she said timidly.

"'I have,' I said, 'and I want you to know the truth. I came because I had to get out of Fall River. I had a scrap - more than one of them.'

"'Did you lick your man?' she said, glancing at me.

"'I licked every one of them, and it was good and fair fighting - if I was on a tear,' I said; 'but I'm ashamed of it now.'

"'You're Larry Moore, who pitched on the Fall Rivers last season?' she said.

"'I am.'

"'You can pitch some!' she said with a nod.

"'When I'm straight I can.'

"'And why don't you go at it like a man then? You could get in the Nationals,' she said.

"'I've never had anyone to work for - before,' I said.

"'We go down here; I'm staying at Keene's boarding-house,' she said at that.

"I was afraid I'd been too forward; so I kept still until we came to the door. Then I pulled off my hat and made her a bow and said: 'Will you let me walk home with you steady, Fanny Montrose?'

"And she stopped on the door-step and looked at me without saying a word, and I asked it again, putting out my hand, for I wanted to get hold of hers. But she drew back and reached for the knob. So I said:

"'You needn't be frightened; for it's me that ought to be afraid.'

"'And what have you to be afraid of, you great big man?' she said, stopping in wonder.

"'I'm afraid of your big black eyes, Fanny Montrose, 'I said, 'and I'm afraid of your slip of a body that I could snap in my hands,' I said; 'for I'm going to fall in love with you, Fanny Montrose.'

"Which was a lie, for I was already. With that I ran off like a fool. I ran off, but from that night I walked home with Fanny Montrose.

"For a month we kept company, and Bill Coogan and Dan Farrar and the rest of them took my notice and kept off. The women laughed at me and sneered at her; but I minded them not, for I knew the ways of the factory, and besides there wasn't a man's voice in the lot - that I heard.

"But one night as we were wandering back to Keene's boarding-house, Fanny Montrose on my arm, Bill Coogan planted himself before us, and called her something to her face that there was no getting around.

"I took her on a bit, weeping and shaking, and I said to her: 'Stand here.'

"And I went back, and caught Bill Coogan by the throat and the belt, and swung him around my head, and flung him against the lamp-post. And the post broke off with a crash, and Coogan lay quiet, with nothing more to say.

"I went back to Fanny Montrose, who had stopped her crying, and said, shaking with anger at the dirty insult: 'Fanny Montrose, will you be my wife? Will you marry me this night?'

"She pushed me away from her, and looked up into my face in a frightened way and said: 'Do you mean to be your wife?'

"'I do,' I said, and then because I was afraid that she didn't trust in me enough yet to marry me I said solemnly: 'Fanny Montrose, you need have no fear. If I've been drunk and riotous, it's because I wanted to be, and now that I've made up my mind to be straight, there isn't a thing living that could turn me back again. Fanny Montrose, will you say you'll be my wife?'

"Then she put out her two hands to me and tumbled into my arms, all limp."

II

Larry Moore rose and walked the length of the room. When he came back he went to the wall and took down a photograph; but with what emotion I could not say, for his back was to me. I glanced again at the odd volatile beauty in the woman's face and wondered what was the word Bill Coogan had said and what was his reason for saying it.

"From that day it was all luck for me," Larry Moore said, settling again in the chair, where his face returned to the shadow. "She had a head on her, that little woman. She pulled me up to where I am. I pitched that season for the Bridgeports. You know the record, Bob, seven games lost out of forty-three, and not so much my fault either. When they were for signing me again, at big money too, the little woman said:

"'Don't you do it, Larry Moore; they're not your class. Just hold out a bit.'

"You know, Bob, how I signed then with the Giants, and how they boosted my salary at the end of that first year; but it was Fanny Montrose who made the contracts every time. We had the child then, and I was happy. The money came quick, and lots of it, and I put it in her lap and said:

"'Do what you want with it; only I want you to enjoy it like a lady.'

"Maybe I was wrong there - maybe I was. It was pride, I'll admit; but there wasn't a lady came to the stands that looked finer than Fanny Montrose, as I always used to call her. I got to be something of a figure, as you know, and the little woman was always riding back and forth to the games in some automobile, and more often with Paul Bargee.

"One afternoon Ed Nichols, who was catching me then, came up with a serious face and said: 'Where's your lady to-day, Larry - and Paul Bargee?' And by the way he said it I knew what he had in mind, and good friend that he was of mine I liked to have throttled him. They told me to pitch the game, and I did. I won it too. Then I ran home without changing my clothes, the people staring at me, and ran up the stairs and flung open the door and stopped and called: 'Fanny Montrose!'

"And I called again, and I called a third time, and only the child came to answer me. Then I knew in my heart that Fanny Montrose had left me and run off with Paul Bargee.

III

"I waited all that night without tasting food or moving, listening for her step on the stairs. And in the morning the postman came without a line or a word for me. I couldn't understand; for I had been a good husband to her, and though I thought over everything that had happened since we'd been married, I couldn't think of a thing that I'd done to hurt her - for I wasn't thinking then of the millions of Paul Bargee.

"In the afternoon there came a dirty little lawyer shuffling in to see me, with blinking little eyes behind his black-rimmed spectacles - a toad of a man.

"'Who are you?' I said, 'and what are you doing here?'

"'I'm simply an attorney,' he said, cringing before my look - 'Solomon Scholl, on a very disagreeable duty,' he said.

"'Do you come from her?' I said, and I caught my breath.

"'I come from Mr. Paul Bargee,' he said, 'and I'd remind you, Mr. Moore, that I come as an attorney on a disagreeable duty.'

" With that I drew back and looked at him in

Owen Johnson

amazement, and said: 'What has he got to say to me?'

"'My client,' he said, turning the words over with the tip of his tongue, 'regrets exceedingly - '

"'Don't waste words!' I said angrily. 'What are you here for?'

"'My client,' he said, looking at me sidelong, 'empowers me to offer you fifteen thousand dollars if you will promise to make no trouble in this matter.'

"I sat down all in a heap; for I didn't know the ways of a gentleman then, Bob, and covered my face with the horror I had of the humiliation he had done me. The lawyer, he misunderstood it, for he crept up softly and whispered in my ear:

"'That's what he offers - if you're fool enough to take it; but if you'll stick to me, we can wring him to the tune of ten times that.'

"I got up and took him and kicked him out of the room, and kicked him down the stairs, for he was a little man, and I wouldn't strike him.

"Then I came back and said to myself: 'If matters are so, I must get the best advice I can.'

"And I knew that Joseph Gilday was the top of the lot. So I went to him, and when I came in I stopped short, for I saw he looked perplexed, and I said: 'I'm in trouble, sir, and my life depends on it, and other lives, and I need the best of advice; so I've come to you. I'm Larry Moore of the Giants; so you may know I can pay.' Then I sat down and told him the story, every word as I've told you; and when I was all through, he said quietly:

"'What are you thinking of doing, Mr. Moore?'

"'I think it would be better if she came back, sir,' I said, 'for her and for the child. So I thought the best thing would be to write her a letter and tell her so; for I think if you could write the right sort of a letter she'd come back. And that's what I want you to show me how to write,' I said.

"He took a sheet of paper and a pen, and looked at me steadily and said: 'What would you say to her?'

"So I drew my hands up under my chin and thought awhile and said: 'I think I'd say something like this, sir:

"""My dear wife - I've been trying to think all this while what has driven you away, and I don't understand. I love you, Fanny Montrose, and I want you to come back to me. And if you're afraid to come, I want to tell you not a word will pass my lips on the subject; for I haven't forgotten that it was you made a man of me; and much as I try, I cannot hate you, Fanny Montrose."'

"He looked down and wrote for a minute, and then he handed me the paper and said: 'Send that.'

"I looked, and saw it was what I had told him, and I said doubtfully: 'Do you think that is best?'

"'I do.'

"So I mailed the letter as he said, and three days after

came one from a lawyer, saying my wife could have no communication with me, and would I send what I had to say to him.

"So I went down to Gilday and told him, and I said: 'We must think of other things, sir, since she likes luxury and those things better; for I'm beginning to think that's it - and there I'm a bit to blame, for I did encourage her. Well, she'll have to marry him - that's all I can see to it," I said, and sat very quiet.

"'He won't marry her,' he said in his quick way.

"I thought he meant because she was bound to me, so I said: 'Of course, after the divorce.'

"'Are you going to get a divorce then from her?'

"'I've been thinking it over,' I said carefully, and I had, 'and I think the best way would be for her to get it. That can be done, can't it?' I said, 'because I've been thinking of the child, and I don't want her to grow up with any stain on the good name of her mother,' I said.

"'Then you will give up the child?' he said.

"And I said: 'Yes.'

"'Will he marry her?' he said again.

"'For what else did he take her away?'

"'If I was you,' he said, looking at me hard, 'I'd make sure of that - before.'

"That worried me a good deal , and I went out and

walked around, and then I went to the station and bought a ticket for Chicago, and I said to myself: 'I'll go and see him'; for by that time I'd made up my mind what I'd do.

"And when I got there the next morning, I went straight to his house, and my heart sank, for it was a great place with a high iron railing all around it and a footman at the door - and I began to understand why Fanny Montrose had left me for him.

"I'd thought a long time about giving another name; but I said to myself: 'No, I'll him a chance first to come down and face me like a man,' so I said to the footman: 'Go tell Paul Bargee that Larry Moore has come to see him.'

"Then I went down the hall and into the great parlor, all hung with draperies, and I looked at myself in the mirrors and looked at the chairs, and I didn't feel like sitting down, and presently the curtains opened, and Paul Bargee stepped into the room. I looked at him once, and then I looked at the floor, and my breath came hard. Then he stepped up to me and stopped and said:

"'Well?'

"And though he had wronged me and wrecked my life, I couldn't help admiring his grit; for the boy was no match for me, and he knew it too, though he never flinched.

"'I've come from New York here to talk with you, Paul Bargee,' I said.

"'You've a right to.'

"'I have,' I said, 'and I want to have an understanding with you now, if you have the time, sir,' I said, and looked at the ground again.

"He drew off, and hearing me speak so low he mistook me as others have done before, and he looked at me hard and said: 'Well, how much?'

"My head went up, and I strode at him; but he never winced - if he had, I think I'd have caught him then and there and served him as I did Bill Coogan. But I stopped and said: 'That's the second mistake you've made, Paul Bargee; the first was when you sent a dirty little lawyer to pay me for taking my wife. And your lawyer came to me and told me to screw you to the last cent. I kicked him out of my sight; and what have you to say why I shouldn't do the same to you, Paul Bargee?'

"He looked white and hurt in his pride, and said: 'You're right; and I beg your pardon, Mr. Moore.'

"'I don't want your pardon,' I said, 'and I won't sit down in your house, and we won't discuss what has happened but what is to be. For there's a great wrong you've done, and I've a right to say what you shall do now, Paul Bargee.'

"He looked at me and said slowly: 'What is that?'

"'You took my wife, and I gave her a chance to come back to me,' I said; 'but she loved you and what you can give better than me. But she's been my wife, and I'm not going to see her go down into the gutter.'

"He started to speak; but I put up my hand and I said: 'I'm not here to discuss with you, Paul Bargee. I've come to say what's going to be done; for I have a child,' I said, 'and I don't intend that the mother of my little girl should go down to the gutter. You've chosen to take my wife, and she's chosen to stay with you. Now, you've got to marry her and make her a good woman,' I said.

"Then Paul Bargee stood off, and I saw what was passing through his mind. And I went up to him and laid my hand on his shoulder and said: 'You know what I mean, and you know what manner of man I am that talks to you like this; for you're no coward,' I said; 'but you marry Fanny Montrose within a week after she gets her freedom, or I am going to kill you wherever you stand. And that's the choice you've got to make, Paul Bargee,' I said.

"Then I stepped back and watched him, and as I did so I saw the curtains move and knew that Fanny Montrose had heard me.

"'You're going to give her the divorce?' he said.

"'I am. I don't intend there shall be a stain on her name,' I said; 'for I loved Fanny Montrose, and she's always the mother of my little girl.'

"Then he went to a chair and sat down and took his head in his hands, and I went out.

IV

"I came back to New York, and went to Mr. Gilday.

"'Will he marry her?' he said at once.

"'He will marry her,' I said. 'As for her, I want you to say; for I'll not write to her myself, since she wouldn't answer me. Say when she's the wife of Paul Bargee I'll bring the child to her myself, and she's to see me; for I have a word to say to her then,' I said, and I laid my fist down on the table. 'Until then the child stays with me.'

"They've said hard things of Mr. Joseph Gilday, and I know it; but I know all that he did for me. For he didn't turn it over to a clerk; but he took hold himself and saw it through as I had said. And when the divorce was given he called me down and told me that Fanny Montrose was a free woman and no blame to her in the sight of the law.

"Then I said: 'It is well. Now write to Paul Bargee that his week has begun. Until then I keep the child, law or no law.' Then I rose and said: 'I thank you, Mr. Gilday. You've been very kind, and I'd like to pay you what I owe you.'

"He sat there a moment and chewed on his mustache,

and he said: 'You don't owe me a cent.'

"'It wasn't charity I came to you for, and I can pay for what I get, Mr. Gilday,' I said. 'Will you give me your regular bill?' I said.

"And he said at last: 'I will.'

"In the middle of the week Paul Bargee's mother came to me and went down on her knees and begged for her son, and I said to her: 'Why should there be one law for him and one law for the likes of me. He's taken my wife; but he sha'n't put her to shame, ma'am, and he sha'n't cast a cloud on the life of my child!'

"Then she stopped arguing, and caught my hands and cried: 'But you won't kill him, you won't kill my son, if he don't?'

"'As sure as Saturday comes, ma'am, and he hasn't made Fanny Montrose a good woman,' I said, 'I'm going to kill Paul Bargee wherever he stands.'

"And Friday morning Mr. Gilday called me down to his office and told me that Paul Bargee had done as I said he should do. And I pressed his hand and said nothing, and he let me sit awhile in his office.

"And after awhile I rose up and said: 'Then I must take the child to her, as I promised, to-night.'

"He walked with me from the office and said: 'Go home to your little girl. I'll see to the tickets, and will come for you at nine o'clock.'

"And at nine o'clock he came in his big carriage, and

Owen Johnson

took me and the child to the station and said: 'Telegraph me when you're leaving to-morrow.'

"And I said: 'I will.'

"Then I went into the car with my little girl asleep in my arms and sat down in the seat, and the porter came and said:

"'Can I make up your berths?'

"And I looked at the child and shook my head. So I held her all night and she slept on my shoulder, while I looked from her out into the darkness, and from the darkness back to her again. And the porter kept passing and passing and staring at me and the child.

"And in the morning we went up to the great house and into the big parlor, and Fanny Montrose came in, as I had said she should, very white and not looking at me. And the child ran to her, and I watched Fanny Montrose catch her up to her breast, and I sobbed. And she looked at me, and saw it. So I said:

"'It's because now I know you love the child and that you'll be kind to her.'

"Then she fell down before me and tried to take my hand. But I stepped back and said:

"'I've made you an honest woman, Fanny Montrose, and now as long as I live I'm going to see you do nothing to disgrace my child.'

"And I went out and took the train back. And Mr. Gilday was at the station there waiting for me, and he took my arm, without a word, and led me to his carriage and drove up without speaking. And when we got to the house, he got out, and took off his hat and made me a bow and said: 'I'm proud to know you, Larry Moore.'"

MY WIFE'S WEDDING PRESENTS

I

I don't believe in wedding functions. I don't believe in honeymoons and particularly I abominate the inhuman custom of giving wedding presents. And this is why:

Clara was the fifth poor daughter of a rich man. I was respectably poor but artistic. We had looked forward to marriage as a time when two persons chose a home and garnished it with furnishings of their own choice, happy in the daily contact with beautiful things. We had often discussed our future home. We knew just the pictures that must hang on the walls, the tone of the rugs that should lie on the floors, the style of the furniture that should stand in the rooms, the pattern of the silver that should adorn our table. Our ideas were clear and positive.

Unfortunately Clara had eight rich relatives who approved of me and I had three maiden aunts, two of whom were in precarious health and must not be financially offended.

I am rather an imperious man, with theories that a woman is happiest when she finds a master; but when the details of the wedding came up for decision I was astounded to find myself not only flouted but actually forced to humiliating surrender. Since then I have learned that my own case was not glaringly exceptional. At the time, however, I was nonplused and rather disturbed in my dreams of the future. I had decided on a house wedding with but the family and a few intimate friends to be present at my happiness. After Clara had done me the honor to consult me, several thousand cards were sent out for the ceremony at the church and an addition was begun on the front veranda.

Clara herself led me to the library and analyzed the situation to me, in the profoundest manner.

"You dear, old, impracticable goose," she said with the wisdom of just twenty, "what do you know about such things? How much do you suppose it will cost us to furnish a house the way we want?"

I said airily, "Oh, about five hundred dollars."

"Take out your pencil," said Clara scornfully, "and write."

When she finished her dictation, and I had added up the items with a groan, I was dumbfounded. I said:

"Clara, do you think it is wise - do you think we have any right to get married?"

"Of course we have."

"Then we must make up our minds to boarding."

"Nonsense! we shall have everything just as we planned it."

"But how?"

"Wedding presents," said Clara triumphantly, "now do you see why it must be a church wedding?"

I began to see.

"But isn't it a bit mercenary?" I said feebly. "Does every one do it?"

"Every one. It is a sort of tax on the unmarried," said Clara with a determined shake of her head. "Quite right that it should be, too."

"Then every one who receives an invitation is expected to contribute to our future welfare?"

"An invitation to the house."

"Well, to the house - then?"

"Certainly."

"Ah, now, my dear, I begin to understand why the presents are always shown."

For all answer Clara extended the sheet of paper on which we had made our calculations.

I capitulated.

II

I pass over the wedding. In theory I have grown more and more opposed to such exhibitions. A wedding is more pathetic than a funeral, and nothing, perhaps, is more out of place than the jubilations of the guests. When a man and a woman, as husband and wife, have lived together five years, then the community should engage a band and serenade them, but at the outset - however, I will not insist - I am doubtless cynically inclined. I come to the moment when, having successfully weathered the pitfalls of the honeymoon (there's another mistaken theory - but let that pass) my wife and I found ourselves at last in our own home, in the midst of our wedding presents. I say in the midst advisably. Clara sat helplessly in the middle of the parlor rug and I glowered from the fireplace.

"My dear Clara," I said, with just a touch of asperity, "you've had your way about the wedding. Now you've got your wedding presents. What are you going to do with them?"

"If people only wouldn't have things marked!" said Clara irrelevantly.

"But they always do," I replied. "Also I may venture to suggest that your answer doesn't solve the difficulty."

"Don't be cross," said Clara.

"My dear," I replied with excellent good-humor, "I'm not. I'm only amused - who wouldn't be?"

"Don't be horrid, George," said Clara.

"It *is* deliciously humorous," I continued. "Quite the most humorous thing I have ever known. I am not cross and I am not horrid; I have made a profound discovery. I know now why so many American marriages are not happy."

"Why, George?"

"Wedding presents," I said savagely, "exactly that, my dear. This being forced to live years of married life surrounded by things you don't want, you never will want, and which you've got to live with or lose your friends."

"Oh, George!" said Clara, gazing around helplessly, "it is terrible, isn't it?"

"Look at that rug you are sitting on," I said, glaring at a six by ten modern French importation. "Cauliflowers contending with unicorns, surrounded by a border of green roses and orange violets - expensive! And until the lamp explodes or the pipes burst we have got to go on and on and on living over that, and why? - because dear Isabel will be here once a week!"

"I thought Isabel would have better taste," said Clara.

"She has - Isabel has perfect taste, depend upon it," I said, "she did it on purpose!"

"George!"

"Exactly that. Have you noticed that married people give the most impossible presents? It is revenge, my dear. Society has preyed upon them. They will prey upon society. Wait until we get a chance!"

"It is awful!" said Clara.

"Let us continue. We have five French rugs; no two could live together. Five rooms desecrated. Our drawing-room is Art Nouveau, furnished by your Uncle James, who is strong and healthy and may live twenty years. I particularly abominate Art Nouveau furniture."

"So do I."

"Our dining-room is distinctly Grand Rapids."

"Now, George!"

"It is."

"Well, it was your Aunt Susan."

"It was, but who suggested it? I pass over the bed-rooms. I will simply say that they are nightmares. Expensive nightmares! I come to the lamps - how many have we?"

"Fourteen."

"Fourteen atrocities, imitation Louis Seize, bogus Oriental, feathered, laced and tasseled. So much for useful presents. Now for decoration. We have three

Sistine Madonnas (my particular abomination). Two, thank heaven, we can inflict on the next victims, one we have got to live with and why? - so that each of our three intimate friends will believe it his own. We have water colors and etchings which we don't want, and a photograph copy of every picture that every one sees in every one's house. Some original friend has even sent us a life-size, marble reproduction of the Venus de Milo. These things will be our artistic home. Then there are vases - "

"Now you are losing your temper."

"On the contrary, I'm reserving it. I shan't characterize the bric-a-brac, that was to be expected."

"Don't!"

"At least that is not marked. I come at last to the silver. Give me the list."

Clara sighed and extended it.

"Four solid silver terrapin dishes."

"Marked."

"Marked - Terrapin - ha! ha! Two massive, expensive, solid silver champagne coolers."

"Marked."

"Marked, my dear - for each end of the table when we give our beefsteak dinners. Almond dishes."

"Don't!"

"Forty-two individual, solid or filigree almond dishes; forty-two, Clara."

"Marked."

"Right again, dear. One dozen bonbon dishes, five nouveau riche sugar shakers (we never use them), three muffineers - in heaven's name, what's that? Solid silver bread dishes, solid silver candlesticks by the dozen, solid silver vegetable dishes, and we expect one servant and an intermittent laundress to do the cooking, washing, make the beds and clean the house besides."

"All marked," said Clara dolefully.

"Every one, my dear. Then the china and the plates, we can't even eat out of the plates we want or drink from the glasses we wish; everything in this house, from top to bottom has been picked out and inflicted upon us against our wants and in defiance of our own taste and we - we have got to go on living with them and trying not to quarrel!"

"You have forgotten the worst of all," said Clara.

"No, my darling, I have not forgotten it. I have thought of nothing else, but I wanted you to mention it."

"The flat silver, George."

"The flat silver, my darling. Twelve dozen, solid silver and teaset to match, bought without consulting us, by your two rich bachelor uncles in collusion. We wanted Queen Anne or Louis Seize, simple, dignified, something to live with and grow fond of, and what did we get?"

Owen Johnson

"Oh, dear, they might have asked me!"

"But they don't, they never do, that is the theory of wedding presents, my dear. We got Pond Lily pattern, repousse until it scratches your fingers. Pond Lily pattern, my dear, which I loathe, detest, and abominate!"

"I too, George."

"And that, my dear, we shall never get rid of; we not only must adopt and assume the responsibility, but must pass it down to our children and our children's children."

"Oh, George, it is terrible - terrible! What are we going to do?"

"My darling Clara, we are going to put a piece of bric-a-brac a day on the newel post, buy a litter of puppies to chew up the rugs, select a butter-fingered, china-breaking waitress, pay storage on the silver and try occasionally to set fire to the furniture."

"But the flat silver, George, what of that?"

"Oh, the flat silver," I said gloomily, "each one has his cross to bear, that shall be ours."

III

We were, as has been suggested, a relatively rich couple. That's a pun! At the end of five years a relative on either side left us a graceful reminder. The problem of living became merely one of degree. At the end of this period we had made considerable progress in the building up of a home which should be in fact and desire entirely ours. That is, we had been extensively fortunate in the preservation of our wedding presents. Our twenty-second housemaid broke a bottle of ink over the parlor rug, her twenty-one predecessors (whom I had particularly selected) had already made the most gratifying progress among the bric-a-brac, two intelligent Airdale puppies had chewed satisfactory holes in the Art Nouveau furniture, even the Sistine Madonna had wrenched loose from its supports and considerately annihilated the jewel-studded Oriental lamp in the general smashup.

Our little home began at last to really reflect something of the artistic taste on which I pride myself. There remained at length only the flat silver and a few thousand dollars' worth of solid silver receptacles for which we had now paid four hundred dollars storage. But these remained, secure, fixed beyond the assaults of the imagination.

One morning at the breakfast table I laid down my cup

with a crash.

Clara gave an exclamation of alarm.

"George dear, what is it?"

For all reply I seized a handful of the Pond Lily pattern silver and gazed at it with a savage joy.

"George, George, what has happened?"

"My dear, I have an idea - a wonderful idea."

"What idea?"

"We will spend the summer in Lone Tree, New Jersey."

Clara screamed.

"Are you in your senses, George?"

"Never more so."

"But it's broiling hot!"

"Hotter than that."

"It is simply deluged with mosquitoes."

"There *are* several mosquitoes there."

"It's a hole in the ground!"

"It certainly is."

"And the only people we know there are the Jimmy Lakes, whom I detest."

"I can't bear them."

"And, George, there are *burglars*!"

"Yes, my dear," I said triumphantly, "heaven be praised there *are* burglars!"

Clara looked at me. She is very quick.

"You are thinking of the silver."

"Of all the silver."

"But, George, can we afford it?"

"Afford what?"

"To have the silver stolen."

"Supposing there was a burglar insurance, as a reward."

The next moment Clara was laughing in my arms.

"Oh, George, you are a wonderful, brilliant man: how did you ever think of it?"

"I just put my mind to it," I said loftily.

IV

We went to Lone Tree, New Jersey. We went there early to meet the migratory spring burglar. We released from storage two chests and three barrels of solid silver wedding presents, took out a burglar insurance for three thousand dollars and proceeded to decorate the dining-room and parlor.

"It looks rather - rather nouveau riche," said Clara, surveying the result.

"My dear, say the word - it is vulgar. But what of that? We have come here for a purpose and we will not be balked. Our object is to offer every facility to the gentlemen who will relieve us of our silver. Nothing concealed, nothing screwed to the floor."

"I think," said Clara, "that the champagne coolers are unnecessary."

The solid silver champagne coolers adorned either side of the fireplace.

"As receptacles for potted ferns they are, it is true, not quite in the best of taste," I admitted. "We might leave them in the hall for umbrellas and canes. But then they might be overlooked, and we must take no chances on a careless burglar."

Clara sat down and began to laugh, which I confess was quite the natural thing to do. Solid silver bread dishes holding sweet peas, individual almond dishes filled with matches, silver baskets for cigars and cigarettes crowded the room, with silver candlesticks sprouting from every ledge and table. The dining-room was worse - but then solid silver terrapin dishes and muffineers, not to mention the two dozen almond dishes left over from the parlor, are not at all appropriate decorations.

"I'm sure the burglars will never come," said Clara, woman fashion.

"If there's anything will keep them away," I said, a little provoked, "it's just that attitude of mind."

"Well, at any rate, I do hope they'll be quick about it, so we can leave this dreadful place."

"They'll never come if you're going to watch them," I said angrily.

We had quite a little quarrel on that point.

The month of June passed and still we remained in possession of our wedding silver. Clara was openly discouraged and if I still clung to my faith, at the bottom I was anxious and impatient. When July passed unfruitfully even our sense of humor was seriously endangered.

"They will never come," said Clara firmly.

"My dear ," I replied, "the last time they came in July. All the more reason that they should change to August."

"They will never come," said Clara a second time.

"Let's bait the hook," I said, trying to turn the subject into a facetious vein. "We might strew a dozen or so of those individual dishes down the path to the road."

"They'll never come," said Clara obstinately.

And yet they came.

On the second of August, about two o'clock in the morning I was awakened out of a deep sleep by the voice of my wife crying:

"George, here's a burglar!"

I thought the joke obvious and ill-timed and sleepily said so.

"But, George dear, he's here - in the room!"

There was something in my wife's voice, a note of ringing exultation, that brought me bolt upright in bed.

"Put up your hands - quick!" said a staccato voice.

It was true, there at the end of the bed, flashing the conventional bull's-eye lantern, stood at last a real burglar.

"Put 'em up!"

My hands went heavenward in thanksgiving and gratitude.

"Make a move, you candy dude, or shout for help," continued the voice, shoving into the light the muzzle of a Colt's revolver, "and this for you's!"

The slighting allusion I took to the credit of the pink and white pajamas I wore - but nothing at that moment could have ruffled my feelings. I was bubbling over with happiness. I wanted to jump up and hug him in my arms. I listened. Downstairs could be heard the sound of feet and an occasional metallic ring.

"Oh, George, isn't it too wonderful - wonderful for words!" said Clara, hysterical with joy.

"I can't believe it," I cried.

"Shut up!" said the voice behind the lantern.

"My dear friend," I said conciliatingly, "there's not the slightest need of your keeping your finger on that wabbling, cold thing. My feelings towards you are only the tenderest and the most grateful."

"Huh!"

"The feelings of a brother! My only fear is that you may overlook one or two articles that I admit are not conveniently exposed."

The bull's-eye turned upon me with a sudden jerk.

"Well, I'll be damned!"

"We have waited for you long and patiently. We thought you would never come. In fact, we had sort of lost faith in you. I'm sorry. I apologize. In a way I don't deserve this - I really don't."

"Bughouse!" came from the foot of the bed, in a suppressed mutter. "Out and out bughouse!"

"Quite wrong," I said cheerily. "I never was in better health. You are surprised, you don't understand. It's not necessary you should. It would rob the situation of its humor if you should. All I ask of you is to take everything, don't make a slip, get it all."

"Oh, do, please, please do!" said Clara earnestly.

The silence at the foot of the bed had the force of an exclamation.

"Above all," I continued anxiously, "don't forget the pots. They stand on either side of the fireplace, filled with ferns. They are not pewter. They are solid silver champagne coolers. They are worth - they are worth - "

"Two hundred apiece," said Clara instantly.

"And don't overlook the muffineers, the terrapin dishes and the candlesticks. We should be very much obliged - very grateful if you could find room for them."

Often since I have thought of that burglar and what must have been his sensations. At the time I was too engrossed with my own feelings. Never have I enjoyed a situation more. It is true I noticed as I proceeded our burglar began to edge away towards the door, keeping the lantern steadily on my face.

"And one favor more," I added, "there are several flocks of individual silver almond dishes roosting downstairs - "

"Forty-two," said Clara, "twenty-four in the dining-room and eighteen in the parlor."

"Forty-two is the number; as a last favor please find room for them; if you don't want them drop them in a river or bury them somewhere. We really would appreciate it. It's our last chance."

"All right," said the burglar in an altered tone. "Don't you worry now, we'll attend to that."

"Remember there are forty-two - if you would count them."

"That's all right - just you rest easy," said the burglar soothingly. "I'll see they all get in."

"Really, if I could be of any assistance downstairs," I said anxiously, "I might really help."

"Oh, don't you worry, Bub, my pals are real careful muts," said the burglar nervously. "Now just keep calm. We'll get 'em all."

It suddenly burst upon me that he took me for a lunatic. I buried my head in the covers and rocked back and forth between tears and laughter.

"Hi! what the - 's going on up there?" cried a voice from downstairs.

"It's all right - all right, Bill," said our burglar hoarsely, "very affable party up here. Say, hurry it up a bit down there, will you?"

All at once it struck me that if I really frightened him too much they might decamp without making a clean sweep. I sobered at once.

"I'm not crazy," I said.

"Sure you're not," said the burglar conciliatingly.

"But I assure you - "

"That's all right."

"I'm perfectly sane."

"Sane as a house!"

"There's nothing to be afraid of."

"Course there isn't. Hi, Bill, won't you hurry up there!"

"I'll explain - "

"Don't you mind that."

"This is the way it is - "

"That's all right, we know all about it."

"You do - "

"Sure, we got your letter."

"What letter?"

"Your telegram then."

"See here, I'm not crazy - "

"You bet you're not," said the burglar, edging towards the door and changing the key.

"Hold up!" I cried in alarm, "don't be a fool. What I want is for you to get everything - everything, do you hear?"

"All right, I'll just go down and speak to him."

"Hold up - "

"I'll tell him."

"Wait," I cried, jumping out of bed in my desire to retain him.

At that moment a whistle came from below and with an exclamation of relief our burglar slammed the door and locked it. We heard him go down three steps at a time and rush out of the house.

"Now you've scared them away," said Clara, "with your idiotic humor."

I felt contrite and alarmed.

"How could I help it?" I said angrily, preparing to climb out on the roof of the porch. "I tried to tell him."

With which I scrambled out on the roof, made my way to the next room and entering, released Clara. At the top of the steps we stood clinging together.

"Suppose they left it all behind," said Clara.

Owen Johnson

"Or even some!"

"Oh, George, I know it - I know it!"

"Don't be unreasonable - let's go down." Holding a candle aloft we descended. The lower floor was stripped of silver - not even an individual almond dish or a muffineer remained. We fell wildly, hilariously into each other's arms and began to dance. I don't know exactly what it was, but it wasn't a minute.

Suddenly Clara stopped.

"George!"

"Oh, Lord, what is it?"

"Supposin'."

"Well - well?"

"Supposin' they've dropped some of it in the path."

We rushed out and searched the path, nothing there. We searched the road - one individual almond dish had fallen. I took it and hammered it beyond recognition and flung it into the pond. It was criminal, but I did it.

And then we went into the house and danced some more. We were happy.

Of course we raised an alarm - after sufficient time to carefully dress, and fill the lantern with oil. Other houses too had been robbed before we had been visited, but as they were occupied by old inhabitants, the occupants had nonchalantly gone to sleep again after surrendering their small change. Our exploit was quite the sensation. With great difficulty we assumed the proper public attitude of shock and despair. The following day I wrote full particulars to the Insurance Company, with a demand for the indemnity.

"You'll never get the full amount," said Clara.

"Why not?"

"You never do. They'll send a man to ask disagreeable questions and to beat us down."

"Let him come."

"You'll see."

Just one week after the event, I opened an official envelope, extracted a check, gazed at it with a superior smile and tendered it to Clara by the tips of my fingers.

"Three thousand dollars!" cried Clara, without contrition, "three thousand dollars - oh, George!"

There it was - three thousand dollars, without a shred of doubt. Womanlike, all Clara had to say was:

"Well, was I right about the wedding presents?"

Which remark I had not foreseen.

We shut up house and went to town next day and began the rounds of the jewelers. In four days we had expended four-fifths of our money - but with what results! Everything we had longed for, planned for, dreamed of was ours and everything harmonized.

Two weeks later as, ensconced in our city house, we moved enraptured about our new-found home, gazing at the reincarnation of our silver, a telegram was put in my hand.

"What is it?" said Clara from the dining-room, where she was fondling our chaste Queen Anne teaset.

"It's a telegram," I said, puzzled.

"Open it, then!"

I tore the envelope, it was from the Insurance Company.

"Our detectives have arrested the burglars. You will be overjoyed to hear that we have recovered your silver in toto!"

THE SURPRISES OF THE LOTTERY

I

The Comte de Bonzag, on the ruined esplanade of his Chateau de Keragouil, frowned into the distant crepuscle of haystack and multiplied hedge, crumpling in his nervous hands two annoying slips of paper. The rugged body had not one more pound of flesh than was absolutely necessary to hold together the long, pointed bones. The bronzed, haphazard face was dominated by a stiff comb of orange-tawny hair, which faithfully reproduced the gaunt unloveliness of generations of Bonzags. But there lurked in the rapid advance of the nose and the abrupt, obstinate eyes a certain staring defiance which effectively limited the field of comment.

At his back, the riddled silhouette of ragged towers and crumbling roof reflected against the gentle skies something of the windy raiment of its owner. It was a Gascon chateau, arrogant and threadbare, which had never cried out at a wound, nor suffered the indignity of a patch. About it and through it, hundreds of swallows, its natural inheritors, crossed and recrossed in their vacillating flight.

Out of the obscurity of the green pastures that melted away into the near woods, the voice of a woman suddenly rose in a tender laugh.

The Comte de Bonzag sat bolt upright, dislodging from his lap a black spaniel, who tumbled on a matronly hound, whose startled yelp of indignation caused the esplanade to vibrate with dogs, that, scurrying from every cranny, assembled in an expectant circle, and waited with hungry tongues the intentions of their master.

The Comte, listening attentively, perceived near the stable his entire domestic staff reclining happily on the arm of Andoche, the Sapeur-Pompier, the hero of a dozen fires.

"No, there are no longer any servants!" he exclaimed, with a bitterness that caused a stir in the pack; then angrily he shouted with all his forces: "Francine! Hey, there, Francine! Come here at once!"

The indisputable fact was that Francine had asked for her wages. Such a demand, indelicate in its simplest form, had been further aggravated by a respectful but clear ultimatum. It was pay, or do the cooking, and if the first was impossible, the second was both impossible and distasteful.

The enemy duly arrived, dimpled and plump, an honest thirty-five, a solid widow, who stopped at the top of the stairs with the distant respect which the Comte de Bonzag inspired even in his creditors.

"Francine, I have thought much," said the Comte, with a conciliatory look. "You were a little exaggerated, but you were in your rights."

"Ah, Monsieur le Comte, six months is long when one has a child who must be - "

"We will not refer again to our disagreement," the Comte said, interrupting her sternly. "I have simply called you to hear what action I have decided on."

"Oh, yes, M'sieur; thank you, M'sieur le Comte."

"Unluckily," said Bonzag, frowning, "I am forced to make a great sacrifice. In a month I could probably have paid all - I have a great uncle at Valle-Temple who is exceedingly ill. But - however, we will hold that for the future. I owe you, my good Francine, wages for six months - sixty francs, representing your service with me. I am going to give you on account, at once, twenty francs, or rather something immeasurably more valuable than that sum." He drew out the two slips of paper, and regarded them with affection and regret. "Here are two tickets for the Grand Lottery of France, which will be drawn this month, ten francs a ticket. I had to go to Chantreuil to get them; number 77,707 and number 200,013. Take them - they are yours."

"But, M'sieur le Comte," said Francine, looking stupidly at the tickets she had passively received. "It's - it's good round pieces of silver I need."

"Francine," cried de Bonzag, in amazed indignation, "do you realize that I probably have given you a fortune - and that I am absolving you of all division of it with me!"

"But, M'sieur - "

Owen Johnson

"That there are one hundred and forty-five numbers that will draw prizes."

"Yes, M'sieur le Comte; but - "

"That there is a prize of one quarter of a million, one third of a million - "

"All the same - "

"That the second prize is for one-half a million, and the first prize for one round million francs."

"M'sieur says?" said Francine, whose eyes began to open.

"One hundred and forty-five chances, and the lowest is for a hundred francs. You think that isn't a sacrifice, eh?"

"Well, Monsieur le Comte," Francine said at last with a sigh, "I'll take them for twenty francs. It's not good round silver, and there's my little girl - "

"Enough!" exclaimed de Bonzag, dismissing her with an angry gesture. "I am making you an heiress, and you have no gratitude! Leave me - and send hither Andoche."

He watched the bulky figure waddle off, sunk back in his chair, and repeated with profound dejection; "No gratitude! There, it's done: this time certainly I have thrown away a quarter of a million at the lowest!"

Presently Andoche, the Sapeur-Pompier, the brass helmet under his arm, appeared at the top of the steps, smiling and thirsty, with covetous eyes fastened on the broken table, at the carafe containing curacoa that was white and "Triple-Sec."

"Ah, it's you, Andoche," said the Comte, finally, drawn from his abstraction by a succession of rapid bows. He took two full-hearted sighs, pushed the carafe slightly in the direction of the Sapeur-Pompier, and added: "Sit down, my good Andoche. I have need to be a little gay. Suppose we talk of Paris."

It was the cue for Andoche to slip gratefully into a chair, possess the carafe and prepare to listen.

Owen Johnson

II

At the proper age of thirty-one, the Comte de Bonzag fell heir to the enormous sum of fifteen thousand francs from an uncle who had made the fortune in trade. With no more delay than it took the great Emperor to fling an army across the Alps, he descended on Paris, resolved to repulse all advances which Louis Napoleon might make, and to lend the splendor of his name and the weight of his fortune only to the Cercle Royale. Two weeks devoted to this loyal end strengthened the Bourbon lines perceptibly, but resulted in a shrinkage of four thousand francs in his own. Next remembering that the aristocracy had always been the patron of the arts, he determined to make a rapid examination of the *coulisses* of the opera and the regions of the ballet. A six-days' reconnaissance discovered not the slightest signs of disaffection; but the thoroughness of his inquiries was such that the completion of his mission found him with just one thousand francs in pocket. Being not only a Loyalist and a patron of the arts, but a statesman and a philosopher, he turned his efforts toward the Quartier Latin, to the great minds who would one day take up the guidance of a more enlightened France. There he made the discovery that one amused himself more than at the Cercle Royale, and spent considerably less than in the arts, and that at one hundred francs a week he aroused an enthusiasm for the Bourbons which almost attained the proportions of a riot.

The three months over, he retired to his estate at Keragouil, having profoundly stirred all classes of society, given new life to the cause of His Majesty, and regretting only, as a true gentleman, the frightful devastation he had left in the hearts of the ladies.

Unfortunately, these brilliant services to Parisian society and his king had left him without any society of his own, forced to the consideration of the difficult problem of how to keep his pipe lighted, his cellar full, and his maid-of-all-work in a state of hopeful expectation, on nothing a year.

Nothing daunted, he attacked this problem of the family bankruptcy with the vigor and the daring of a D'Artagnan. Each year he collected laboriously twenty francs, and invested them in two tickets for the Great Lottery, valiantly resolved, like a Gascon, to carry off both first and second prizes, but satisfied as a philosopher if he could figure among the honorable mentions. Despite the fact that one hundred and forty-five prizes were advertised each year, in nineteen attempts he had not even had the pleasure of seeing his name in print. This result, far from discouraging him, only inflamed his confidence. For he had dipped into mathematics, and consoled himself by the reflection that, according to the law of probabilities, each year he became the more irresistible.

Lately, however, one obstacle had arisen to the successful carrying out of this system of finance. He employed one servant, a maid-of-all-work, who was engaged for the day, with permission to take from the garden what she needed, to adorn herself from the rose-bushes, to share the output of La Belle Etoile, the cow, and to receive a salary of ten francs a month. The difficulty invariably arose over the interpretation of this last clause. For the Comte was not regular in his payments, unless it could be said that he was regular in not paying at all.

So it invariably occurred that the maid-of-all-work from a state of unrest gradually passed into open rebellion, especially when the garden was not productive and the roses ceased to bloom. When the ultimatum was served, the Comte consulted his resources and found them invariably to consist of two tickets of the Lottery of France, cash value twenty francs, but, according to the laws of probability, increasingly capable of returning one million, five hundred thousand francs. On one side was the glory of the ancient name, and the possibility of another descent on Paris; opposed was the brutal question of soup and ragout. The man prevailed, and the maid-of-all-work grudgingly accepted the conditions of truce. Then the news of the drawing arrived and the domestic staff departed.

This comedy, annually repeated, was annually played on the same lines. Only each year the period intervening between the surrender of the tickets and the announcement of the lottery brought an increasing agony. Each time as the Comte saw the precious slips finally depart in the hands of the maid-of-all-work, he was convinced that at last the laws of probability must fructify. Each year he found a new meaning in the cabalistic mysteries of numbers. The eighteenth attempt, multiplied by three, gave fifty-four, his age. Success was inevitable: nineteen, a number indivisible and chaste above all others, seemed specially designated. In a word, the Comte suffered during these periods as only a gambler of the fourth generation is able to suffer.

At present the number twenty appeared to him to have properties no other number had possessed, especially in the reappearance of the zero, a figure which peculiarly attracted him by its symmetry. His despair was consequently unlimited.

Ordinarily the news of the lottery arrived by an inspector of roads, who passed through Keragouil a week or so after the announcement in the press; for the Comte, having surrendered his ticket, was only troubled lest he had won.

This time, to the upsetting of all history, an Englishman on a bicycle trip brought him a newspaper, an article almost unknown to Keragouil, where the shriek of the locomotive had yet to penetrate.

The Comte de Bonzag, opening the paper with the accustomed sinking of the heart, was startled by the staring headlines:

RESULTS OF THE LOTTERY

A glance at the winners of the first and second prizes reassured him. He drew a breath of satisfaction, saying gratefully; "Ah, what luck! God be praised! I'll never do that again!"

Then, remembering with only an idle curiosity the one hundred and forty-three mediocre prizes on the list, he returned to the perusal. Suddenly the print swam before his eyes, and the great esplanade seemed to rise.

Number 77,707 had won the fourth prize of one hundred thousand francs; number 200,013, a prize of ten thousand francs.

III

The emotion which overwhelmed Napoleon at Waterloo as he beheld his triumphant squadrons go down into the sunken road was not a whit more complete than the despair of the Comte de Bonzag when he realized that the one hundred and ten thousand francs which the laws of probability had finally produced was now the property of Francine, the cook.

One hundred and ten thousand francs! It was colossal! Five generations of Bonzags had never touched as much as that. One hundred and ten thousand francs meant the rehabilitation of the ancient name, the restoration of the Chateau de Keragouil, half the year at Paris, in the Cercle Royale, in the regions of art, and among the great minds that were still young in the Quartier - and all that was in the possession of a plump Gascony peasant, whose ideas of comfort and pleasure were satisfied by one hundred and twenty francs a year.

"What am I going to do?" he cried, rising in an outburst of anger. Then he sat down in despair. There was nothing to do. The fact was obvious that Francine was an heiress, possessed of the greatest fortune in the memory of Keragouil. There was nothing to do, or rather, there was manifestly but one way open, and the

Comte resolved on the spot to take it. He must have back the lottery tickets, though it meant a Comtesse de Bonzag.

Fortunately for him, Francine knew nothing of the arrival of the paper. Though it was necessary to make haste, there was still time for a compatriot of D'Artagnan. There was, of course, Andoche, the Sapeur-Pompier; but a Bonzag who had had three months' experience with the feminine heart of Paris was not the man to trouble himself over a Sapeur-Pompier. That evening, in the dim dining-room, when Francine arrived with the steaming soup, the Comte, who had waited with a spoon in his fist and a napkin knotted to his neck, plunged valiantly to the issue.

"Ah, what a good smell!" he said, elevating his nose. "Francine, you are the queen of cooks."

"Oh, M'sieur le Comte," Francine stammered, stopping in amazement. "Oh, M'sieur le Comte, thanks."

"Don't thank me; it is I who am grateful."

"Oh, M'sieur!"

"Yes, yes, yes! Francine - "

"What is it, M'sieur le Comte?"

"To-night you may set another cover - opposite me."

"Set another cover?"

"Exactly."

Francine, more and more astonished, proceeded to place on the table a plate, a knife and a fork.

"M'sieur le Cure is coming?" she said, drawing up a chair.

"No, Francine."

"Not M'sieur le Cure? Who, then?"

"It is for you, Francine. Sit down."

"I? I, M'sieur le Comte?"

"Sit down. I wish it."

Francine took three steps backward and so as to command the exit, stopped and stared at her master, with mingled amazement and distrust.

"My dear Francine," continued the Comte, "I am tired of eating alone. It is bad for the digestion. And I am bored. I have need of society. So sit down."

"M'sieur orders it?"

"I ask it as a favor, Francine."

Francine, with open eyes, advanced doubtfully, seating herself nicely on the chair, more astonished than complimented, and more alarmed than pleased.

"Ah, that is nicer!" said the Comte, with an approving nod. "How have I endured it all these years! Francine, you may help yourself to the wine."

The astonished maid-of-all-work, who had swallowed a spoon of soup with great discomfort, sprang up, all in a tremble, stammering with defiant virtue:

"M'sieur le Comte does not forget that I am an honest woman!"

"No, my dear Francine; I am certain of it. So sit down in peace. I will tell you the situation."

Francine hesitated, then, reassured by the devotion he gave to his soup, settled once more in her chair.

"Francine, I have made up my mind to one thing," said the Comte, filling his glass with such energy that a red circle appeared on the cloth. "This life I lead is all wrong. A man is a sociable being. He needs society. Isolation sends him back to the brute."

"Oh, yes, M'sieur le Comte," said Francine, who understood nothing.

"So I am resolved to marry."

"M'sieur will marry!" cried Francine, who spilled half her soup with the shock.

"Perfectly. It is for that I have asked you to keep me company."

"M'sieur - you - M'sieur wants to marry me!"

"Parbleu!"

"M'sieur - M'sieur wants to marry me!"

"I ask you formally to be my wife."

"I?"

"M'sieur wants - wants me to be Comtesse de Bonzag?"

"Immediately."

"Oh!"

Springing up, Francine stood a moment gazing at him in frightened alarm; then, with a cry, she vanished heavily through the door.

"She has gone to Andoche," said the Comte, angrily to himself. "She loves him!"

In great perturbation he left the room promenading on the esplanade, in the midst of his hounds, talking uneasily to himself.

"*Peste*, I put it to her a little too suddenly! It was a blunder. If she loves that Sapeur-Pompier, eh? A Sapeur-Pompier, to rival a Comte de Bonzag - faugh!"

Suddenly, below in the moonlight, he beheld Andoche tearing himself from the embrace of Francine, and, not to be seen, he returned nervously to the dining-room.

Shortly after, the maid-of-all-work returned, calm, but with telltale eyes.

"Well, Francine, did I frighten you?" said the Comte, genially.

"Oh, yes, M'sieur le Comte - "

"Well, what do you want to say?"

"M'sieur was in real earnest?"

"Never more so."

"M'sieur really wants to make me the Comtesse de Bonzag?"

"*Dame!* I tell you my intentions are honorable."

"M'sieur will let me ask him one question?"

"A dozen even."

"M'sieur remembers that I am a widow - "

"With one child, yes."

"M'sieur, pardon me; I have been thinking much, and I have been thinking of my little girl. What would M'sieur want me to do?"

The Comte reflected, and said generously: "I do not adopt her; but, if you like, she shall live here."

"Then, M'sieur," said Francine, dropping on her knees, "I thank M'sieur very much. M'sieur is too kind, too good - "

"So, it is decided then," said the Comte, rising joyfully.

"Oh, yes, M'sieur."

"Then we shall go to-morrow," said the Comte. "It is my manner; I like to do things instantly. Stand up, I beg you, Madame."

"To-morrow, M'sieur?"

"Yes, Madame. Have you any objections?"

"Oh, no, M'sieur le Comte; on the contrary," said Francine, blushing with pleasure at the twice-repeated "Madame." Then she added carefully: "M'sieur is quite right; it would be better. People talk so."

IV

The return of the married couple was the sensation of Keragouil, for the Comte de Bonzag, after the fashion of his ancestors, had placed his bride behind him on the broad back of Quatre Diables, who proceeded with unaltered equanimity. Along the journey the peasants, who held the Comte in loyal terror, greeted the procession with a respectful silence, congregating in the road to stare and chatter only when the amiable Quatre Diables had disappeared in the distance.

Disdaining to notice the commotion he produced, the Comte headed straight for the courtyard, where Quatre Diables, recognizing the foot block, dropped his head and began to crop the grass. The new Comtesse, fatigued by the novel position, started gratefully to descend by the most natural way, that is, by slipping easily over the rear anatomy of the good-natured Quatre Diables. But the Comte, feeling the commotion behind, stopped her with a word, and, flinging his left leg over the neck of his charger, descended gracefully to the block, where, bowing profoundly, he said in gallant style:

"Madame, permit me to offer you my hand."

The Comtesse, with the best intentions in the world, had considerable difficulty in executing the movement by which her husband had extricated himself. Luckily, the Comte received her without yielding ground, drew her hand under his arm, and escorted her ceremoniously into the chateau, while Quatre Diables, liberated from the unusual burden, rolled gratefully to earth, and scratched his back against the cobblestones.

"Madame, be so kind as to enter your home."

With studied elegance, the Comte put his hat to his breast, or thereabout, and bowed as he held open the door.

"Oh, M'sieur le Comte; after you," said Francine, in confusion.

"Pass, Madame, and enter the dining-room. We have certain ceremonies to observe."

Francine dutifully advanced, but kept an eye on the movements of her consort. When he entered the dining-room and went to the sideboard, she took an equal number of steps in the same direction. When, having brought out a bottle and glasses, he turned and came toward her, she retreated. When he stopped, she stopped, and sat down with the same exact movement.

"Madame, I offer you a glass of the famous Keragouil Burgundy," began the Comte, filling her glass. "It is a wine that we De Bonzags have always kept to welcome our wives and to greet our children. Madame, I have the honor to drink to the Comtesse de Bonzag."

"Oh, M'sieur le Comte," said Francine, who, watching his manner, emptied the goblet in one swallow.

"To the health of my ancestors!" continued the Comte, draining the bottle into the two goblets. "And now throw your glass on the floor!"

"Yes, M'sieur," said Francine, who obeyed regretfully, with the new instinct of a housewife.

"Now, Madame, as wife and mistress of Keragouil, I think it is well that you understand your position and what I expect of you," said the Comte, waving her to a seat and occupying a fauteuil in magisterial fashion. "I expect that you will learn in a willing spirit what I shall teach you, that you may become worthy of the noble position you occupy."

"Oh, M'sieur may be sure I'll do my best," said Francine, quite overcome.

"I expect you to show me the deference and obedience that I demand as head of the house of Bonzag."

"Oh, M'sieur le Comte, how could you think - "

"To be economical and amiable."

"Yes, indeed, M'sieur."

"To listen when I speak, to forget you were a peasant, to give me three desserts a week, and never, madame, to show me the slightest infidelity."

At these last words, Francine, already overcome by the rapid whirl of fortune, as well as by the overcharged spirits of the potent Burgundy, burst into tears.

"And no tears!" said De Bonzag, withdrawing sternly.

"No, M'sieur; no," Francine cried, hastily drying her eyes. Then dropping on her knees, she managed to say: "Oh, M'sieur - pardon, pardon."

"What do you mean?" cried the Comte, furiously.

"Oh, M'sieur forgive me - I will tell you all!"

"Madame - Madame, I don't understand," said the Comte, mastering himself with difficulty. "Proceed; I am listening."

"Oh, M'sieur le Comte, I'll tell you all. I swear it on the image of St. Jacques d'Acquin."

"You have not lied to me about your child?" cried Bonzag in horror.

"No, no, M'sieur; not that," said Francine. Then, hiding her face, she said: "M'sieur, I hid something from you: I loved Andoche."

"Ah!" said the Comte, with a sigh of relief. He sat down, adding sympathetically: "My poor Francine, I know it. Alas! That's what life is."

"Oh, M'sieur, it's all over; I swear it!" Francine cried in protest. "But I loved him well, and he loved me - oh, how he loved me, M'sieur le Comte! Pardon, M'sieur, but at that time I didn't think of being a comtesse, M'sieur le Comte. And when M'sieur spoke to me, I didn't know what to do. My heart was all given to Andoche, but - well, M'sieur, the truth is, I began to think of my little girl, and I said to myself, I must think of her, because, M'sieur, I thought of the position it would give her, if I were a Comtesse. What a step in the world, eh? And I said, you must do it for her! So I went to Andoche, and I told him all - yes, all, M'sieur - that my heart was his, but that my duty was to her. And Andoche, ah, what a good heart, M'sieur - he understood - we wept together." She choked a minute, put her handkerchief hastily to her eyes, "Pardon, M'sieur; and he said it was right, and I kissed him - I hide nothing, M'sieur will pardon me that, - and he went away!" She took a step toward him, twisting her handkerchief, adding in a timid appeal: "M'sieur understands why I tell him that? M'sieur will believe me. I have killed all that. It is no more in my heart. I swear it by the image of St. Jacques d'Acquin."

"Madame, I knew it before," said the Comte, rising; "still, I thank you."

"Oh, M'sieur, I have put it all away - I swear it!"

"I believe you," interrupted the Comte, "and now no more of it! I also am going to be frank with you." He went with a smile to a corner where stood the little box, done up in rope, which held the trousseau of the Comtesse de Bonzag. "Open that, and give me the lottery-tickets I gave you."

"Hanh? You - M'sieur says?"

"The lottery-tickets - "

"Oh, M'sieur, but they're not there - "

"Then where are they?"

"Oh, M'sieur, wait; I'll tell you," said Francine, simply. "When Andoche went off - "

"What!" cried the Comte, like a cannon.

"He was so broken up, M'sieur, I was so afraid for him, so just to console him, M'sieur - to give him something - I gave him the tickets."

"You gave him - the tickets! The lottery-tickets!"

"Just to console him - yes, M'sieur."

The lank form of the Comte de Bonzag wavered, and then, as though the body had suddenly deserted the clothes, collapsed in a heap on the floor.

Choose from Thousands of 1stWorldLibrary Classics By

Adolphus William Ward
Aesop
Agatha Christie
Alexander Aaronsohn
Alexander Kielland
Alexandre Dumas
Alfred Gatty
Alfred Ollivant
Alice Duer Miller
Alice Turner Curtis
Alice Dunbar
Ambrose Bierce
Amelia E. Barr
Andrew Lang
Andrew McFarland Davis
Anna Sewell
Annie Besant
Annie Hamilton Donnell
Annie Payson Call
Anton Chekhov
Arnold Bennett
Arthur Conan Doyle
Arthur Ransome
Atticus
B. M. Bower
Basil King
Bayard Taylor
Ben Macomber
Booth Tarkington
Bram Stoker
C. Collodi
C. E. Orr
C. M. Ingleby
Carolyn Wells
Catherine Parr Traill
Charles A. Eastman
Charles Dickens
Charles Dudley Warner
Charles Farrar Browne
Charles Ives
Charles Kingsley
Charles Lathrop Pack
Charles Whibley
Charles Willing Beale
Charlotte M. Braeme
Charlotte M.Yonge
Clair W. Hayes
Clarence Day Jr.
Clarence E. Mulford

Clemence Housman
Confucius
Cornelis DeWitt Wilcox
Cyril Burleigh
D. H. Lawrence
Daniel Defoe
David Garnett
Don Carlos Janes
Donald Keyhole
Dorothy Kilner
Dougan Clark
E. Nesbit
E.P.Roe
E. Phillips Oppenheim
Edgar Allan Poe
Edgar Rice Burroughs
Edith Wharton
Edward J. O'Brien
John Cournos
Edwin L. Arnold
Eleanor Atkins
Elizabeth Cleghorn
Gaskell
Elizabeth Von Arnim
Ellem Key
Emily Dickinson
Erasmus W. Jones
Ernie Howard Pie
Ethel Turner
Ethel Watts Mumford
Eugenie Foa
Eugene Wood
Evelyn Everett-Green
Everard Cotes
F. J. Cross
Federick Austin Ogg
Ferdinand Ossendowski
Francis Bacon
Francis Darwin
Frances Hodgson Burnett
Frank Gee Patchin
Frank Harris
Frank Jewett Mather
Frank L. Packard
Frederick Trevor Hill
Frederick Winslow Taylor
Friedrich Kerst
Friedrich Nietzsche
Fyodor Dostoyevsky

Gabrielle E. Jackson
Garrett P. Serviss
Gaston Leroux
George Ade
Geroge Bernard Shaw
George Ebers
George Eliot
George MacDonald
George Orwell
George Tucker
George W. Cable
George Wharton James
Gertrude Atherton
Grace E. King
Grant Allen
Guillermo A. Sherwell
Gulielma Zollinger
Gustav Flaubert
H. A. Cody
H. B. Irving
H. G. Wells
H. H. Munro
H. Irving Hancock
H. Rider Haggard
H. W. C. Davis
Hamilton Wright Mabie
Hans Christian Andersen
Harold Avery
Harold McGrath
Harriet Beecher Stowe
Harry Houidini
Helent Hunt Jackson
Helen Nicolay
Hendy David Thoreau
Henrik Ibsen
Henry Adams
Henry Ford
Henry Frost
Henry James
Henry Jones Ford
Henry Seton Merriman
Henry Wadsworth
Longfellow
Henry W Longfellow
Herbert A. Giles
Herbert N. Casson
Herman Hesse
Homer
Honore De Balzac

Horace Walpole
Horatio Alger, Jr.
Howard Pyle
Howard R. Garis
Hugh Lofting
Hugh Walpole
Humphry Ward
Ian Maclaren
Israel Abrahams
J.G.Austin
J. Henri Fabre
J. M. Barrie
J. Macdonald Oxley
J. S. Knowles
J. Storer Clouston
Jack London
Jacob Abbott
James Allen
James Lane Allen
James Andrews
James Baldwin
James DeMille
James Joyce
James Oliver Curwood
James Oppenheim
James Otis
Jane Austen
Jens Peter Jacobsen
Jerome K. Jerome
John Burroughs
John F. Kennedy
John Gay
John Glasworthy
John Habberton
John Joy Bell
John Milton
John Philip Sousa
Jonathan Swift
Joseph Carey
Joseph Conrad
Joseph Jacobs
Julian Hawthrone
Julies Vernes
Justin Huntly McCarthy
Kakuzo Okakura
Kenneth Grahame
Kate Langley Bosher
L. A. Abbot
L. T. Meade
L. Frank Baum
Laura Lee Hope

Laurence Housman
Leo Tolstoy
Leonid Andreyev
Lewis Carroll
Lilian Bell
Lloyd Osbourne
Louis Tracy
Louisa May Alcott
Lucy Fitch Perkins
Lucy Maud Montgomery
Lydia Miller Middleton
Lyndon Orr
M. H. Adams
Margaret E. Sangster
Margaret Vandercook
Maria Edgeworth
Maria Thompson Daviess
Mariano Azuela
Marion Polk Angellotti
Mark Overton
Mark Twain
Mary Austin
Mary Cole
Mary Rowlandson
Mary Wollstonecraft
Shelley
Max Beerbohm
Myra Kelly
Nathaniel Hawthrone
O. F. Walton
Oscar Wilde
Owen Johnson
P.G.Wodehouse
Paul and Mable Thorn
Paul G. Tomlinson
Paul Severing
Peter B. Kyne
Plato
R. Derby Holmes
R. L. Stevenson
Rabindranath Tagore
Rahul Alvares
Ralph Waldo Emmerson
Rene Descartes
Rex E. Beach
Richard Harding Davis
Richard Jefferies
Robert Barr
Robert Frost
Robert Gordon Anderson
Robert L. Drake

Robert Lansing
Robert Michael Ballantyne
Robert W. Chambers
Rosa Nouchette Carey
Ross Kay
Rudyard Kipling
Samuel B. Allison
Samuel Hopkins Adams
Sarah Bernhardt
Selma Lagerlof
Sherwood Anderson
Sigmund Freud
Standish O'Grady
Stanley Weyman
Stella Benson
Stephen Crane
Stewart Edward White
Stijn Streuvels
Swami Abhedananda
Swami Parmananda
T. S. Ackland
The Princess Der Ling
Thomas A. Janvier
Thomas A Kempis
Thomas Anderton
Thomas Bailey Aldrich
Thomas Bulfinch
Thomas De Quincey
Thomas H. Huxley
Thomas Hardy
Thomas More
Thornton W. Burgess
U. S. Grant
Valentine Williams
Victor Appleton
Virginia Woolf
Walter Scott
Washington Irving
Wilbur Lawton
Wilkie Collins
Willa Cather
Willard F. Baker
William Makepeace
Thackeray
William W. Walter
Winston Churchill
Yei Theodora Ozaki
Young E. Allison
Zane Grey

www.ingramcontent.com/pod-product-compliance
Lightning Source LLC
Chambersburg PA
CBHW030112180626
46812CB00002B/381